Resolution

Cherry Tree Heights

J. Haney
S.I. Hayes

This novel is entirely a work of fiction. Names, characters, businesses, places, events, and incidents are either the products of the author's imagination or used in a fictitious manner. Any resemblance to actual persons, living or dead, or actual events is purely coincidental.

No part of this book may be reproduced or transmitted in any form or by any means, electronic or mechanical, including mechanical photocopying, recording, or any information storage and retrieval system, without permission in writing.

Cover Design by S.I. Hayes

Haney Hayes Promotions

Copyright © 2021 Haney /Hayes

ISBN:

ALL RIGHTS RESERVED.

Chapter 1- Winnie

Just another Saturday night without kids at Sweet'ums. It's owned by one of my best friends. Brenton Sweet is the oldest of our little group, and he opened Sweet'ums seven years ago when his daughter Clara was eight. He's also the only one out of the little group besides myself that smokes.

"Has Clara started on you about quitting?" I ask, taking another drag off my cigarette.

He exhales, and a minty vapor envelopes us. "Not really. She's more about wanting to get her own. Wants to try the dessert flavors." He takes another drag. "I keep telling her not until she's old enough to buy it herself, which just tells me she's hiding one somewhere in her panty drawer. You wanna come over and look?"

RESOLUTION

"Why am I the one that gets asked to do these things? I had to go to Piper's when the boys were like fifteen because she didn't know how to give them *the sex talk*, and all of you were too chicken shit." I roll my eyes.

"So tomorrow, then?" He laughs. "I'm afraid since I found her B.O.B. in her nightstand. That led to a very long uncomfortable talk last fall."

"Yeah, Brent, I'll be there tomorrow around lunch. You better have a good meal ready for me, though. Got me?" I ask, putting out my cigarette.

"You know, I will. I'm grabbing a beer. You want another watermelon vodka?"

"Please, I'm going to see if everyone's still seated and not dancing on the tables."

He goes on ahead of me and beelines for the bar as I head for the table. I barely get seated before Piper starts.

"Win, you really stink. You need to quit that nasty habit already."

"I'm *trying*. It's hard to do when nothing else is working," I whine. I make a face at Piper. Piper O'Reilly and I have known one another for years. Hated each other from first sight in Kindergarten when she decided to take my seat in Miss Bush's class. It was because I was smaller. I was a late bloomer. I also didn't take much shit from anyone. I pulled her pretty pink bow from her head-hair and all. We didn't start getting along till high school when we found out a boy was playing us both. Best friends since. "Are the boys ready for school to start back on Monday?"

"Of course not. Jeremiah and Clara were talking about it when I left them at the coffee shop." Piper says. Not only does she own Sweet Caroline's, she's got twin seventeen-year-old boys. Isaiah and Jeremiah.

I laugh. "Dante and Jeremiah, were busy watching Micah do some kind of mermaid thing on one of the regulars."

"I've got everything in place, lunch boxes ready to be filled, and backpacks stuffed. I tell ya, I love them, but the girls have run me ragged this break. I never should have taken them up to Universal. Now all Dante wants to do is make monsters out of them, and they're inclined to let him! There's Karo syrup and chocolate sauce all over my kitchen! *Why?* Because it makes the best blood!" Bryce Blackmon sucks down his bourbon with exasperation. Bryce is a mortician, which still gives me the creeps. He-like Austin and me- has three kids. Dante is fifteen and twin seven-year-old girls Rumor and Echo.

"Want to trade? I spent break with basketball for all three, volleyball and dance for the girls, and Crew decided he was going to get a *girlfriend*, so I took him on his first date last night." My head hits the table.

"But he's *twelve*..." Austin Doyle looks at me, horrified. "Ashton's at the house right now with him. I'm not ready for little girls after his peen. It's too soon." Speaking of Austin Doyle. His son Ashton is ten and closest to my Crew at twelve. He's also got the most adorable twin three-year-old girls Allyson and Addyson. I swear there is something in the water.

RESOLUTION

"Like they were yours? Have you started having the talk with him?" I pick up my head curiously.

"He's *ten*! If I have that talk with him, he's gonna have it with Ivy and Iris, and Rumor and Echo, and everyone else that will listen. I'll be getting the call from the school. You know him. He doesn't shut the hell up." Austin shakes his head.

"He doesn't repeat anything I tell him not to. I swear that's just you." I chuckle.

"Me either, I've let words slip, and he doesn't tattle or say them," Tatum speaks up. She was on the phone. Being the youngest of the group and no children makes her the D.D. No stress and all. She also works with me at Winnie's Wonder Salon and Spa.

"Me, his mother, I swear Felica teaches him a new set of cusses every week." Felicia is Austin's baby momma. They never married, but boy can they reproduce.

"Oh, just wait till he's as big as you and tries the real back talk. Dante pulled that shit with me the other night, and I was like, *boy, you better take the bass outta your voice*." Bryce chuckles. "Kid may be six foot two, but I'll still level his ass if he keeps smartin' off."

"How are the girls not all over him? He's adorable and knows his stuff." Tatum smirks.

"Fortunately, for me, I think they think he's gay. He's always so busy messing with his sketches or building new makeups that he doesn't look up to see them. I mean, we've had that talk, sort of. I even bought him condoms since school started. I'm not ready to be a grandpa yet, ya know?" He looks around. "Where the fuck did Brenton get up to?"

"He was supposed to be getting us drinks?" I stand up looking. "Looks like another blonde bimbo. I'll be right back. Time to cock block because he ain't messing with our one night out." I walk away from the table and beeline for Brent and the blonde bimbo. "Baby, there you are. We've all been waiting on you." I wrap my hand over his shoulder.

He stiffens up, his head on a swivel as he hears my voice. "Winnie?" He smiles. "You're just in time. Young Tia here was just about to show me her tattoo." He looks back, and the bimbo is fixing her dress and picking up her drink. "Awe come on. It ain't like that." He whines as she shrugs and walks away. "You a horrible wingman. Now, who's gonna slob my knob tonight?"

"Call me a hater if you want to. Say I'm trippin' if you feel like. I can bet it won't be me!" I sing-song, taking my drink and skipping back to the table.

"Skip-skip, skip to my loo, skip to my loo, my darlin'!" Comes from the guys as I approach.

"He's got such a puss on his face." Bryce chuckles.

"No, see, that's the problem, no *puss* on his face." Austin snickers.

"Guess he better learn to suck himself." I snort.

"Winnie! What did you do?" Tatum asks.

RESOLUTION

"Nothing, I swear."

"Bullshit!" Comes from Piper. "Nothing like when Brad Jenks played the two of us, and you posted naked pictures of him all over the school?"

"I wouldn't have done that." I bat my lashes.

"You would, and I'm pretty sure Brenton can suck is his own junk. Clara got all that flexibility from someone," Austin says, getting up. "Be right back. Gotta piss."

"Don't be picking up no bimbos. I mean. We are not here for sex tonight!"

"Oh, I don't know what happens at Sweet'ums stays at Sweet'ums." He winks at me, walking away.

"Nope! I have no idea what you are referring to!"

Chapter 2- Jarrett

My little girl really is all grown up. Married just a little over a year, and already she's about to make a grandfather of me. Five months from now, I'm going to be holding Scott Windom Brooks-Guteriez. I know a mouthful for such a little person, but Sofia, my daughter, hyphenated because she's my one and only baby. She wanted to make sure the Brooks name carries on. I laughed at her when she said it, but she's got a point. Twenty-five years and no other kids. Hell, no other really serious relationships. My world has been Sofia. Always has been, always will be.

The baby shower is one of those new-fangled hybrid things. You know the ones where the food is trendy, and mommy and daddy get together and do something goofy to reveal the baby's gender? Yeah, they went with water balloons.

RESOLUTION

They had white shirts on and black balloons pre-filled with the corresponding color. So now my little girl is covered in blue and happy as a lark. Me? Where am I? Oh, just out on the balcony of this Boston Highrise, freezing my nuts off to get away from the masses and sneak a smoke.

I hear the glass door open and shut quickly, followed by a sigh.

"Daddy? What are you doing?

Flicking my butt, I blow out the smoke quickly. *Busted.* I turn around. "Hi. baby."

Sofia frowns at me. "You were smoking?"

"I- no- it's just this icy January air." I blow hot breath. "See?"

"Your lighter is right there on the railing." Her hands go to her quickly swelling belly. "You *promised.*"

"I made a resolution to try and quit. There's a difference. It's only been five days. Give a man a break. I haven't bought a pack since coming out here. That's progress."

"No. That's you being cheap." She comes over and hugs me. "We both know you order online and stashed a carton in your suitcase for the weekend."

I smooth down her long black hair. "You know your daddy too well."

"Promise me. Promise me you'll quit before this baby comes. I don't want anything to happen to you, like grams and gramps. I want you to be able to *play* with him, not be chained to an oxygen machine till you give up the ghost."

I sigh. She would guilt me. My little girl has learned the art of the guilt trip. "When are you coming home to Cherry Hill?" I try and change the subject.

"Daddy?" Sofia shoves me. "Promise!"

"Okay! I promise I'm gonna try my best."

"Fine, Fillipe just needs to finalize the paperwork for his transfer, and we'll be back. Should be a couple of weeks at most."

"Okay. A couple of weeks. I can make progress in a couple of weeks."

***

Home. Cherry Tree Heights, California. If San Francisco and Beverly Hills had a baby, Cherry Tree Heights would be the result. Not far from the clifftop shores of Brighton Beach, the community is about ten-thousand strong. I own a nice four-bedroom up down about fifteen minutes from downtown and ten from the beach. Since Sofia moved out three years ago, it's just been me, and if it wasn't for all the memories in the place, I'd have sold it off long ago.

I order a pizza and some wings before sitting down to catch a playoff game. I don't have a team- I just root for everyone- *not* the New England Patriots. That shit with the deflated balls is just unforgivable. I'm packing down my third slice of meat-lovers when my phone rings.

"Yeah?" I answer, still chewing.

"You wanna maybe swallow before talkin' there, big guy?" I hear the silvery tongue of Gabriella, my *ex-wife*.

RESOLUTION

"Gabby? Hi." I say, leaning into the edge of my seat. I wipe my mouth and my hands like she can see me.

"So, how's our little girl? I was sorry I couldn't make the trip out with you. My job wouldn't give me the time off."

"Yeah, she's good. They're having a boy. Calling him Scott."

"Oh, how wonderful." She's quiet a moment. "What are you doing?"

"Nothing, having some dinner."

"Oh? What's on the menu?"

"Pizza, hot wings, and beer." I chuckle.

"Hmm, no dessert?" She purrs, and I can almost pop my jeans for the hardon it gives me. She's got this voice on her and the way she rolls her tongue... *No. Stop Jarrett.* This woman is a man-eater. She's chewed you up and spit you out on more than one occasion over the years. The very reason you can't seem to get on solid ground with any other woman is because of this one.

"*Gabby...*" My doorbell rings. "J- just a sec!" I holler. "Hold on. Someone's at my door." I go to the door and swing it open to find Gabby in the doorway in just panties, bra, heels, and stockings with a jacket over top.

"Dessert is *served*." She wraps her arms around my neck, and we tumble into the house. The door slams behind us, and she's on me like a cat on a rat. My clothes are made fast work of, and she barely kisses me before I feel my cock surrounded by her tight hot pussy.

"Uh-Gabby," I question, and she puts her hand over my mouth.

"Shut up." She growls, reaching back and grabbing my balls with her free hand. Her heels dig into my legs as she bounces up and down on my cock. It's hard and fast and just what I need after a long weekend in a cold state. Falling down, so we're chest to chest, she pumps on me, my hands on her still firm ass. This woman may be pushing fifty, but her workouts keep her tight as a drum.

A few figure eights, and she's mewling like a strangled cat. I always hated this part. Her coming is like listening to nails on a chalkboard. If she wasn't so fucking talented with her body, I'd probably never come. Speaking of which, I blow my load, and she collapses alongside me. One thing I'm grateful for was her getting fixed. She made that decision all on her own, and it's made our little trysts a whole lot easier. It also made sure Sofie stayed an *only* child.

"What are you doing here?" I ask, still panting, my heart still racing.

"Just came for my bi-monthly nut." She rolls on top of me, kisses me, and shoves off to stand. "See you in March." She wraps her coat around her teeny form and lets herself out.

"Fuck." I let my head hit the hardwood. "I need a smoke."

RESOLUTION

Chapter 3- Winnie

School weeks kill me. Summer and holidays are so much easier. Every morning and afternoon, not only do I have my own three, Crew, who's turning thirteen. The twins Iris and Ivy will be ten. I have Austin's three Mondays and Fridays but just Allyson and Addyson Tuesday through Thursday and Bryce's Rumor and Echo. Bryce handles lunch for all kids, and Austin gets breakfast, leaving me to be the taxi and handle after school snack and dinner.

I dropped off the two sleeping angels to Austin, and we ended up carrying them up to bed. He's just going to bathe them in the morning. Ballet wore them out today. Good thing we always pack lounging clothes for after school.

Parking in Bryce's driveway, all the kids bounce out and help carry stuff in. Rumor and

Echo have a full schedule, just like my kids. Lunch boxes and bags in hand, the kids make their way to the door. I'm falling behind, and Bryce is at the door by the time I get there, and the kids have disappeared.

"You look like you could use a glass of wine." He smiles, leaning in the doorway.

"I need something. The girls had a new experience today, and I wasn't ready for it."

He pushes the door open further. Wanna come in and talk about it?" He looks over his shoulder, no kids in sight. "Or would you rather I pick you up in say two hours?" His voice is low and husky, just how I like it.

"That would be *just* what I could use, but Ivy got a friend today for the first time at school. Needless to say, I'm cleaning the laundry. So, unless you plan to help with that, I don't think anything is going on today, Stud."

"I'm sure I could work you over through the rinse cycle." He steps into my space just as Crew appears, making him step back again.

"Mom, can we go? I need to call Melanie before she goes to bed." Crew says, and I can't help but roll my eyes. Melanie is the *girlfriend*.

"Yeah, Crew, grab your sisters while I talk to Bryce."

"*Fine*." He says with a full attitude walking away.

"How'd you do this with Dante?"

"Well, I *was* bigger than him. He doesn't give me lip. I've shown him the results of runaways, drunk drivers, and drug addicts. He's too scared to really step out of line."

I shove against his chest. "That's horrible!"

"But effective. I was real with him, he wanted to start his crazy, and I showed him where it could lead him. Now he's about hard work and film school. Working and learning from your girls at the salon. Girls are a distant second-hell- maybe even a third or fourth for him."

"Must be nice. All I've heard is, *do you think Melanie and I will get married? Do you think we'll make pretty babies?* Seriously, I thought it was the girls I'd have to worry about."

"You need to nip it now, our you'll be a grandmother before he gets out of junior high. Winnie, these kids need you to put your foot down. You know it too. Do you want me to pull a file? Show him what can happen to a girl his age if she has a baby?"

"No, God, No! It would be different if Brad was around more than once a year. I'm trying to find the balance."

"*Mom!*" Crew whines sisters underarms.

"Go to the car. I'm coming." I pull the kids out the door. "Guess that's our cue."

He leans back into his place in the doorway. "I'll be up for a while if you find yourself with some time to spare."

"I can't leave the house tonight." I shake my head. "I'll see you in the morning. Add chocolate to Ivy's lunch."

"I'll add it Iris' too, and you should pack her with stuff, if Ivy's got it, Iris isn't far behind."

"Neither is Rumor and Echo. They're all together every day. See you later." I wave, heading for the car.

***

I'm on my way to see a hypnotherapist. See Crew, and I made a deal. I will try this out, and he'll cool it with the girlfriend. I'm walking into the office. It's small and quiet, even with the kids sitting in the corner playing. I stop at reception.

"Name, please?" The guy behind the counter asks.

"Winnie, McCormick. I'm here to see Doctor Holloway."

"We'll just need you to fill out some new patient forms. I'll also need your I.D. and insurance."

"Sure thing." I pull the cards out of my purse and hand them to the guy.

He hands me the cards back with all the forms I have to fill out. "Just fill everything out and bring it back up when you're finished. They'll come get you when they're ready for you. If you'll just sign for insurance."

I smile, signing and take the forms sitting down. Adding a piece of gum to my mouth, my leg starts going a million miles a minute as I start on all the forms.

"I swear they ask all the same shit on the online forms before you even get here." A deep voice half whispers, startling me out of my paperwork fog.

RESOLUTION

"There were online forms? Christ!" I grumble, getting another piece of gum.

"Careful, you'll wind up with lockjaw." I see movement near me, and a hand extended. "Jarrett, Salems are my downfall. You?"

I put my hand in his. "Winnie, Marlboro menthol light one hundreds and fruity vapes."

"Ahh, see, I know a nic fit when I see one. I was you last week. Chewed through a whole pack of Bubbleyum before Doctor Halloway came out. Made myself sick as a dog for two days."

I look the guy over. He's in jeans, a tee-shirt, and mucky work boots. Here I am in my Winnie's Wonder Salon and Spa tee with a pair of mom jeans. I'm not even positive were washed before I threw them on.

"If I get sick, I'll get a break and kids off my back about smoking." I smile at him.

"You too? Let me guess Christmas or New Year's, right? Made you promise?" He chuckles, looking me over. "Winnie's? You own it or just a coincidental name?"

"Depends. Was your experience good or bad?"

"I do this do all by myself. Rarely have time to go to a barber, let alone a shmancy salon like you run."

"Don't knock till you try it. We're open from eight am till eleven pm every day. My girls could do a number on you."

"Well, if I go, I'd expect the best, so who's your best team?" He smiles at me, and before I can answer, a tall man pops his head out of a door.

"Jarrett? You ready?"

Jarrett shrugs, "Maybe some other time." Picking up his hat, he nods at me standing.

"Ask for me, and if I'm not there, tell them Winnie said to show you the works. They'll understand." Fuck me, he's tall! Keep yourself together, Winnie.

"I may just do that." He answers. "It was nice meeting you." With that, he disappears behind the door.

Chapter 4- Jarrett

A blur. That's what my second session with the therapist today has been. Francis Halloway explained what I needed to do to prepare for my first hypnosis treatment, and I couldn't tell you word one about it. I was too busy wondering about the blue-eyed gal in the waiting room. Winnie. The name doesn't suit her. She's more of a Samantha or Indigo, maybe even a Camilla. Something bold to offset the soft baby girl's voice that comes out of her pouty little mouth.

She's younger than me, that's for sure, but not so young as to have Sofia scolding me. I get out of the office, hoping to run into her, but I couldn't just wait around. I had no business there and doing so just to see her may come off as creepy and stalkerish. Instead, I head out and immediately Google Winnie's Salon and Spa.

Hundreds of hits. The place was opened about three years ago and shot off like a Roman candle. She's got celebrities from all over that flock to the place for a day of relaxation and pampering. Lord knows I could use a bit of all that and then some. Maybe I'll eke out some time this week.

My phone rings as I pull up to the property I'm working on right now. See, I'm a House Flipper. I buy up real estate in bad shape, and with some elbow grease and a bit of help, I manage to renovate and sell at a substantial profit.

"Hello?"

"Daddy?" My little girl's sniffling.

"Baby? What's the matter?" I turn off the ignition.

"Fillipe- he-he-" She sobs. "We had a fight."

"Where are you?" I growl. "Did he hurt you?"

She sniffles and sobs again. "I'm- I'm okay. I'm at a hotel, daddy, come get me?"

"I'm already there." I try to hold my tongue— that rat bastard. "I'm booking a flight. Text me where you are."

***

A five and half hour flight takes me right into Boston for just a quarter past five. I hate jumping time zones. It always fucks me up. I don't have time to bother trying to adjust. My baby needs me. She cries, and my heart breaks always has. I may not have carried her or brought her into this world, but she's still the best part of me in this world. Gabby and I may not have gotten the marriage or divorced thing right, but we sure did make one wonderful woman. I get a cab to the Hilton downtown and head straight up to room ten- twenty-two. I didn't bother to pack, as I don't plan to stay. I'm getting Sofia, and we're getting out of this frozen tundra of a state.

I knock and watch as she looks through the peephole. The door opens, and there stands my baby. She's wearing yoga pants and an oversized tee-shirt with her hair down and in her face. She flings herself at me, wrapping her little arms around me as she sobs.

"I'm sorry, daddy."

"Baby, there's nothing to be sorry for." I look down at her as she looks up at me. Her face has a large bruise across it, and she seems to have bitten through her lip partly. It's been cleaned up, but still. This is my baby, and someone has laid their filthy hands on her. "Where is he?"

"I-I just wanna go home. With you. Daddy, *please*. I was afraid to fly alone, or I'd have just come already."

I tilt her head up and see the yellowed bruising around her neck. It looks like finger marks and maybe a ring. "How long has he been doing this?"

Sofia looks away, pulls away. Her hands-on her belly. "I thought he was gonna stop. He promised no more rough stuff. You know because of the baby?"

"Sofia, *how* long?" I demand.

"Since the beginning. Since we got married. Before he was sweet and tender, then it was like a switch got flipped."

My blood is boiling. I am seeing red. I taste blood from chewing my cheeks.

"*Daddy, please.* Just get me out of here. Get *us* out of here." She grasps my forearms with her tiny hands. "*Please.*"

I lick my lips to bring the moisture back to them, along with the salt from the sweat that's broken out on me. I nod. "Do you have anything with you?"

"No, Daddy. I took off as soon as he headed for the shower. I used my emergency credit card to get the room."

"Okay. I'll get us a flight back home. You go lay down. After the ordeal you've been through, you need to rest." She curls up on the king-sized bed and pulls the blankets over her head. I take the phone out into the hallway and call the airport. The earliest flight back I can get is at seven tomorrow morning. I guess I'm taking a nap. I sit on the bed, and I guess she feels my body displace the mattress because in seconds, she's curled up against me, just like when she was a little girl, and the thunder would send her crying into my arms.

I don't sleep. I'm too hyper-aware that she's been hurt, that there's a distinct possibility that baby could be hurt. How long had he choked her? It was obviously hard enough. What can oxygen deprivation to the mother do to a baby? Unable to shut these thoughts off, I pull out my phone. The hotel's got Wi-Fi to use, so I fall down the Quora and March Of Dimes rabbit holes. Talks about the cycle of abuse, the women that continue to go back. How a lack of oxygen can

RESOLUTION

cause birth defects like Cerebral Palsy and heat disease. Cause premature birth, low weight, it all makes me rather sick to my stomach. I pull my baby into me and just hold her until my eyes cross, and I finally pass out.

Chapter 5- Winnie

"I don't care who's driving tonight, but I can promise you it won't be me." I say, taking my seat at the table.

"That bad, huh?" Tatum asks.

"Where did these kids pick up that I should quit smoking? And why did it have to be the week my nine-year-olds both start their period?" I drop my head to the table as both Tatum and Piper being howling with laughter.

"Do I have to start throwing massive amounts of suckers and candy bars at you to keep from fearing for my life?" Austin asks, sitting down with the first round of drinks. "Brenton is dealing with a late shipment in back. He's gonna be a while."

Bryce gives me a look of pity and understanding.

"Suck it, Austin," I say, looking at the menu.

RESOLUTION

"Are you actually like cigarette free tonight?" Bryce asks, watching me. He takes a sniff. "I'd say no, by the amount of perfume you've got on to mask the smell."

"I've not had one in twenty-four hours. There was an issue at work, and I had to go in. Needless to say, the woman didn't like that scent after she'd had it for four months. Bitch threw the bottle at me, and it busted."

"Here, drink up." Austin puts a shot of vodka and a blue electric lemonade in front of me.

"Trying to get me shit faced?"

"You just said you need it, so I'm giving up mine. Shut up and drink it." He drops his vodka and slams the shot glass on the table. Grabbing Tracie, one of the waitresses, he smirks. "Bring us two rounds of purple motherfuckers. It's a kidless night!"

Two hours later and our table is full of shot glasses. I think we're all on birth control, or at least I hope we all are. I'm not sure we can handle any more kids in this group right now. I found Brenton earlier, and we discussed my twin problem after he laughed for a solid twenty minutes. I left the table a bit ago to go to the bar but found myself in the bathroom, throwing water on my face. I needed to sober up some before finding the biggest guy in the place and wrapping myself around him in the back hall. I won't say I've done it before, but I also won't say I haven't.

I'm straightening my top as I'm coming out of the bathroom. Jesus, I still smell like a French whore. I should have gone home showered and changed, but then I would have been the D.D. and fuck tha-What the fuck? I fall forward as someone bumps into me.

"Christ almighty," I say, climbing back to my feet as hands wrap around my arms. "I'm fine," I say, dusting myself off. "Thank you." That's when I hear a huh sort of snicker sort of chuckle all at once.

"Hello again." I turn around and see the guy from therapy. If I thought I looked bad Tuesday, I'm looking horrible now.

"Jarrett, right? Sorry, I'm sort of clumsy sometimes."

"Seems like it." He smiles. "What are you- I mean, are you here with friends or?" He trails off, looking toward the dining room.

"A friend of mine owns the place. It's a Saturday night ritual. Kids with the babysitter and a few of us get together."

"Oh, that must be nice after a long week." He looks down at the floor a second or two. "You should probably get back. I should probably-" He points toward the dining room, whereas we're all outside. "It was nice seeing you again."

"Yeah, you too." I wave and head toward the group that is now watching me very intently. That was awkward as all fuck. I can't help but look for him through the glass as I sit down. He's in the dining room with a woman. A pregnant one at that. It seems he likes them young, like Bradley.

"Who was that?" Piper asking breaking me from the fog I seem to be in.

RESOLUTION

"Just some guy I met the other day," I answer nonchalantly.

Bryce shifts in his chair, but it's Brent that speaks.

"Which one? I didn't see it."

"It doesn't matter. He's here with someone. Quit being so obvious!"

"It's the silver fox over there with the pregnant chick. His knees almost touch the table. Damn, Win, could you imagine what wrapping around that would be like?" Piper speaks up.

"DRINK!" I shout, and all eyes round toward me.

Brent laughs. "You don't recognize the girl?" He nudges me. "Look again. That's Sofie Brooks, one of the best damn waitresses I ever had. You were trying to mount her *father*."

"I wasn't trying to mount nobody! We chatted while sitting at the doctor's, okay? Then he knocked me over, coming out of the bathroom. Christ!"

"Mmhmm." Austin and Brent say together. Bryce is just looking at me with a smile that says I'm gonna be his tonight.

Fuck. It's always like this. Bryce turns into a horn dog, and I fall into bed with him or the back seat of his car. I can't keep doing that. I deserve something more than a romp.

"That's it, I've had enough. I'm taking Uber home. Austin, my kids are staying at your place. Have fun with the girl's crazy. I'll see you tomorrow to come get them and my car." I stand, grabbing my purse.

"You sure?" Bryce goes to stand. He's been nursing the same beer all night. "I can get you home." He tosses a twenty on the table for Tracie.

"Oh, I'm sure you can get her home." Tatum elbows Piper, who does the same to Brent.

"Yeah, I think I need a night to soak in the tub and forget all my problems."

Bryce comes around the table as I stumble back. "Woman, you can't hardly walk. I've got you. My car's a helluva lot closer than Tatum's or the bench for an Uber."

"I'll be fine once I get some food into me," I grumble as he takes my arm, leading me away from the group.

"You've been eating all night, so it's not a *food* you're craving." We walk through the parking lot, and there's his 1974 Ford Bronco, painstakingly restored in some weirdly named paint. It looks blue to me. It reminds me of the kind of jeep surfers should be attaching their gear to down Brighton Beach. I will say this though, those frame bars are great to hold onto.

"How do you know what I'm craving?" I ask as he helps me into the passenger seat.

"Because you've been marinating for hours." He tilts my head back as he straps me in. "I'm just the tall drink of water you ordered." He kisses me, and I melt against him for a moment.

"Not here, take me home, in a bed, and fuck me senseless."

He needs no further prompting. Seconds later, he's in the driver's seat, and we're headed for my now empty house.

Chapter 6- Jarrett

Another Tuesday, another day with Doctor Holloway. After the drama of bringing Sofia home, I need to decompress to someone. My session is supposed to be two-fold. Thirty minutes with Francis and thirty minutes with Gene. One psychoanalyzes while the other does the *actual* hypnotherapy. I'm not sure if I buy into it all, but I'm trying. For Sofia, for little Scotty. With a protective order in place, I'm all they really have.

I'm sitting in the waiting room, early as usual, when the door dings. I look up, and there is Winnie. She's in this lightweight sheer pale purple top with a tank underneath and dark slim-fit jeans you'd expect to see paired with strappy heels, but not this girl. Nope, she's in a pair of low cut purple Chuck Taylors. I can't help but smile as she goes over to the reception desk and checks in.

They appear to be giving her some grief, as the look on her pretty pale face is one of stress. She starts for her bag on the counter and oomph. Thunk. Over it goes, little bottles rolling everywhere! The guy behind the desk just watches as she audibly swears, dropping to the floor to chase her belongings.

I'm up and grabbing the things that have rolled in my direction. It looks like shampoos and lotions. Weird, but um, okay. Guess it's better than dildos and condoms. I had that happen with a girl one time. Not sure what she had in store for me that night, but I didn't stick around to find out. I walk over to her, still gathering her things to her in a pile.

"You are really selling this clumsy shtick."

She looks up at me, pulling her lip into her mouth with her teeth. "I told you I was." She's just tossing stuff in her bag. I hand down the little bottles I have.

"It gets better," I assure her, offering my hand to help her up.

"Thank you." She says, letting me help her to her feet. "You're going to start thinking I'm stalking you like some crazy woman."

I look around. "Think it's safe to say we both got a screw or two loose. I mean hypnosis?" I chuckle. "Wouldn't you love to just go outside to that little roach coach, grab a sub-par coffee and suck one down?"

"If I knew my kid wouldn't smell it and call me on my shit, yes. He's determined I need to quit now. I don't know why this time, but I was able to get something I wanted out of it. So, I'm trying."

"Oh, me too. They've got me tapering down, though; they say it's the most effective route with how long I've been at it." I walk with her to the waiting area. "Trust me, cold turkey, and I with a nail gun wouldn't go over well for anyone." I half-laugh as we sit.

"About the same as me cutting someone's hair." She cringes. "I could imagine the damage I'd do." She pulls a notepad and pen from her bag with one of the bottles.

"What's that you're doing? May I ask?" I lean into her. Her scent is spicy this time. Last week it was more of a citrus smell.

"I'm starting my own line of products, so I have to go through tester samples to find the ones I like best."

"That must be exciting for you." Her own line. Impressive. She's motivated, at least.

"My girls love the idea. I'm starting to think it could be more trouble than it's worth. Like the shampoos, if I like the scent, I hate how it makes my hair look."

"Are you using essential oils? I mean, if you do, you should be able to get the company to mix the blends and get you the scents you want in the formulas you need."

"That's what they say, but it's not looking like it. Here try this, it's supposed to be a lotion for men, but I think it's girly."

I take the little bottle and uncap it, putting a little on my hand. I rub it in. "It feels nice, but umm-" I take a sniff. "Too much rosehips and not enough amber."

"Do I even want to know how you know this?" She asks, jotting down notes.

I laugh. "Single dad of a very creative young woman. Sofie was into everything she could sign up for, from scouts to powderpuff football. She took me along for the ride. You should see my hobby room."

"Sounds like my kids, Crew is into everything you'd expect a boy to be into, plus he plays sax. The girls, though, they may be the death of me. They have the most, I think, followed Crew into Martial Arts and band. Ivy has the flute, and Iris is all about the drums."

"Sofie took the cello. It was crazy; it was almost as big as she is. She was good. Offered the first chair in the California Symphony, but decided to marry instead." I get quiet. Little did I know that the son of a bitch, Fillipe was the real reason.

"I remember her from her time at Sweet'ums. I thought she moved to the east coast. Congratulations on becoming a papaw."

Before I can respond, Francis comes out. "Jarrett?" Damnit.

"Yeah? One sec." I turn back to Winnie, pulling out my wallet. I fish through it and find one of my business cards with my number on it. "I gotta go but call me sometime. We can get lunch or something."

She swaps me the card for a piece of paper. "Bring Sofie in to be pampered one day." She smiles at me. I take the paper and, with a nod,

RESOLUTION

follow Francis. I know where I'm going, so I check out the scrap of paper. On it is her number and the words; *Took you long enough.*

Chapter 7- Winnie

Disgruntled customers, they really suck. Especially when they are in the wrong and everyone knows it.

"Missus Johnson, it shows that Evan has done your hair, Michele handled your nails, and Dante rang up your purchase of three hundred and fifty. Counting all the services and products you picked up. So I'm having trouble understanding what the problem was."

"That boy rang the stuff up for double what it was."

I hear the chime of the door without looking up, I call. "Welcome to Winnie's, have a look around, and we'll be with you momentarily." I look back at the thorn in my side for the moment. "I'm looking at the receipt now. Nothing was rung up double what it was supposed to be. You changed up your products this time."

RESOLUTION

"Are you sure?" Missus Johnson asks.

"Positive If you would like to exchange them, we can do that. Also, you let them know your next cut is on me. I'll even make note of it for whoever has it right here on the system."

"That won't be necessary. Thank you, Winnie."

"You're quite welcome. Have a great day and thank you for choosing Winnie's."

Just as she walks away, *Shoop* by Salt N Peppa plays over the speakers, and Evan pulls me to the middle of the floor with him. Are we dancing? Oh yeah, breaking it down old school while we sing along.

I hear a chuckle, and looking up, I see who our newest victims-er-customers are. Sofie and Jarrett Brooks. As the song ends, I make my way over to them.

"Welcome to Winnie's. Can I offer you a cut and style? Mani, Pedi? Wax, massage, or tan? Sauna? You name it, and we offer it, and if we don't, then I'm not doing my job right."

"Daddy?" Sofie looks up at her father like any girl would.

"Whatever you want, baby, so long as it's safe for you two." Jarrett nods. "I was told I needed the works?" He smiles at me, and I swear I feel my face flush.

'Who do you want to work on you? Man, woman, no preference?"

"Whoever can make me not feel like a louse." Sofie answers.

I look at her, and my smile almost falters as I see the markings on her neck. "So, then let's do the Mommy package for you. That gets everything you can think of and more. The best part it's all safe for you and your little one. If you just follow Keristen, she'll get you in a robe and start you out with a prenatal massage. If you need anything, just ask Keristen, and she will make it happen."

"Thank you." She smiles sheepishly, looking to her dad for the nod.

"Go on; you wanted a spa day." He waves her away, then trains his eye on me. "You got an opening? Or do I have to wait my turn?"

"Let me just check." I click around on the computer for a second. "Seems you're in luck. We had a cancelation. I'm free till two-thirty."

"So, what can you do for me in two and a half hours?" He touches the overgrowth on his face thoughtfully.

"Depends on what you want, but we can get a lot done in that time frame. Just follow Dylan, and he'll get you set up."

"Sounds like a plan. Let's rock n' roll."

Dylan takes Jarret one way, and I head for the massage room. I didn't learn all of this for nothing. My back is to the door when it opens.

"Robe off, and the towel should be draped over you. Get comfortable and let me know when you are."

"So you're trained to do all this? Or is it some nifty ploy to get me naked and at your mercy?" He asks as I hear the table shift and him grunt a bit. "Front or back first?"

"Completely up to you. We'll do fifteen minutes on both sides. Oh, and you can tell me *after* if I know what I'm doing or not. Preference on scent and noise?"

I hear a chuckle. "Um, seeing as this will be my first professionally given massage, I'll leave it to you, as you would know best. Just don't use anything eucalyptus, as I'm allergic to it. I'm good to go."

"Sandalwood, okay?" I turn, looking over at him. He's lying on his back watching me. "Need a pillow?"

"No. I think I'm good." He watches me from the table. "Sandalwood is good, too."

I grab the sandalwood oil and bring it over with me. I start with his face. "Just let me know if something bothers you."

"Trust me if you hurt me. I'll let you know." He closes his eyes, and I get to work.

At first, it's me working on him. No talking, just a lot of breathing, and I swear the tension in this room is through the roof. I'm working on his chest, which has me leaned over him. He lets out a giggle, and I have to steady myself with his abs because I wasn't ready for it.

"You laugh a lot."

"I'm ticklish." He clears his throat. "And your hands are really smooth."

"Did you expect them to be hard?"

Again with the clearing of the throat. "I don't know what I expected. I didn't-don't expect anything." He opens his eyes, looking up at me. "I'm just accustomed to my own scaly hands, I guess."

"But this isn't so bad, is it?" I ask, moving from his chest to his abs and stomach. He shifts.

"It's *different*."

"Just something new. New experiences are always good." I snort as The *Humpty Dance* by Digital Underground starts playing. His whole body contracts as he starts full-on belly laughing.

"I-I can't-this music it's-too much!"

"You don't like the Humpty Dance?" I ask and dance around a little.

"All I see is that guy with the thing on his nose. It was horrible, then, it's horrible now."

"You just don't know what fun is," I say. "Ready for me to work your legs and feet?"

"My *feet*? You really wanna make a man laugh till he chokes, don't you?" He sits up on his elbows, putting us nearly nose to nose. "How's about we skip the feet? I don't wanna kick out and inadvertently flash you my junk."

"Wouldn't be the first time that happened, and I'm sure it won't be the last. What about your legs? Do you want me to work them, or do you want to skip to your back?"

"Let's do the back. The only people that have seen my junk aside from doctors had damn good reason to. Anything else is an unnecessary tease."

"I'm going to move away and turn around. You let me know when you're fixed." I say, looking at him one last time before I start to get down.

A moment of grunting and a bit of creaking comes from the table. "Alrighty. I think I got it." I turn, and he's got his arms above his head, and his face, which should be in the donut, is resting on them. "You're not like gonna jump on me like some trained housecat, are you? Like they do in the movies."

"Is that what you want?" I ask with a laugh.

He's quiet a moment before turning his head toward me. "That depends on how well you can knead, and will there be a tongue bath involved?"

"Is that what you're into? Pussy cats?" What the fuck am I saying. Shut up, Winnie. You're going to make yourself look even more stupid than you already have. "Anyway, I'm going to have to um well staddle you to get the right leverage on your back. If that's okay?" Yup, my face is flaming.

He looks straight ahead, "Do what you gotta do. Do you need a hand getting up?"

"I think I've got it. You just relax and try not to throw me off if I tickle you."

Another throat clear. "Done."

"Do you need something for your throat? I'm sure we have something around here."

"Nope, must be the oils, or perhaps my aggressive need for a smoke."

I swallow, getting up on the stool and getting ready to straddle this man that has been invading my dreams. To make it worse, Saturday, when I let Bryce take me home and fuck me stupid, I saw this man's face.

"Um, I can see where that would bother you. It does me. I usually don't do the massages unless someone asks for me."

He shifts as my hands roam down his tight muscular back. For an older man, his physique is better than guys half his age. He turns his head, and I notice that there are just the beginnings of salting in his otherwise dark brown hair.

"I have a pack of Salem's in my jeans over there. I'm betting the incense would totally cover up the smoke smell."

With my legs on either side of his hips, I run my hands up his back from his ass to his neck. "You're killing me, Mister Brooks."

"That wasn't a no."

Chapter 8- Jarrett

"Ohh..." Winnie exhales, leaning against me on the table. I've corrupted her into breaking a few state laws. She blows a smoke ring watching it sail up into the ventilation system.

"It's good, right?" I watch as her crossed leg swings back and forth.

"Oh, yeah, I'd rank it right there next to sex."

My smile widens before I take another drag. "If this is as good as the sex you're getting, then you've got a lazy lover." I exhale, watching her. I've still not gotten dressed and am sitting beside her with just the towel wrapped neatly around my waist.

"I'm divorced."

"That makes two of us. So now that we've established our lack of spouses, how's about you let me take you to lunch? Say tomorrow, while your kids are still in school?"

"I can probably let you do that, but I'll meet you wherever."

"Fair enough. I'm working out by Brighton Beach. I assume you know the area?" She nods at me. "How about we meet at Kirby's Krab shack? Get a couple of lobster rolls, maybe an ice cream?"

"Yeah, I can handle that. Around noon or one?"

"I'm flexible." I ash into the little sand-filled incense burner. The tension is not as thick as it was when she was touching me, but there's definitely something in the air between us.

"Even being the size of a man that you are?" She answers, and then her eyes widen when she catches what she said. "Ignore me. I have no idea what's come over me." She turns a lovely shade of red.

Just as I'm about to say something cheeky, the door opens. Winnie jumps from the table and almost face plants as I'm dousing out the cigarette.

"Sorry, Win-thought, you were out. The session should have ended ten minutes ago," Keristen says, not even attempting to curb her smile as my daughter looks on from behind her.

"We were just finishing. Um-Just a few more minutes cleaning up the oil that I spilled, and he needs to dress since I'm-er-he needs a cut and trim."

RESOLUTION

"Sure thing. We'll just go over to the courtyard for a little relaxing mediation." Keristen lowers her head and closes the door.

Winnie's chest heaves, and I can't help but imagine how it would feel pressed passionately against mine. I hop down from the table, grabbing my pants and shorts. Licking my lips before I speak, I look at her as she intently watches me.

"It's closed now, that window of opportunity. Though I think we can both agree we've just had a moment."

"I'll agree there was something." I watch as her body shakes, and she turns from me. "I-I'm just going to wipe this down, and then you can get dressed." She gets to work, and I pull it together.

Following her out of the massage room, we return to the center of the shop, where she sets me into a chair and gets to washing my hair. She doesn't talk, at least not to me. A couple of her employees say one thing or another, and she just massages my scalp. It's relaxing, and the warm water is nice. Just as is the hot towel, she wraps around my face before leaving me there, without much more than an *I'll be back*. Great, so I've turned her into our past Governor.

I must have fallen asleep because the next thing I know, I'm being smacked by my daughter. "Ow." I jibe as my eyes adjust, and I'm looking at someone, *not* Winnie.

"Hi, Winnie had to run, but I was told to take great care of you. I'm Ginger." The twenty-something with perky tits and flaming red and blonde hair smiles as she puts out her hand. Apparently, I am unable to school my disappointment as she purses her lips. "I'm really good at edging. You'll be pleased. I promise."

I get up. "I hope it wasn't anything serious."

"Eh, schools call, she runs." Ginger answers. "It's what happens when you're at the top of the phone tree."

***

Sofie and I finished dinner a couple of hours ago. I had to try to get her to believe that Winnie and I weren't doing anything too scandalous. I'm sure she doesn't believe me, and it's to that effect that I did not tell her about the little lunch date I made. Whether she would be for or against it isn't the issue, it's just I don't want to flaunt anything like this in her face, especially with her talking to a lawyer about a divorce.

I take a shower and wash the oils Winnie rubbed all over me away. Her hands are so small, delicately painted perfectly pink. I wonder if she has a pedicure to match. I'm not really a foot guy, but I like a woman that pulls themselves together in the little ways. I mean, I don't care if she's in ratty sweats with a two-day-old messy bun. If her hands and feet are matched up, I'm a goner.

I need to get up by four-thirty, but there's no sleep to be found. I lay in my bed and stare at the clock watching the numbers tick by. I reach for my phone and my wallet. Pulling out the little scrap of paper Winnie gave me, I take a deep breath. Here goes nothing.

"Crew, it's fine. Just go to bed. Sorry, hello?"

RESOLUTION

I hear her messing in the background. Shit, I flaked-its bedtime. "I- uh-" I panic and hang up. Christ. What am I twelve? She's got caller I.D., you idiot! The phone rings in my hand, and I toss it across the room. I can hear her on the other side. What the fuck? Seriously? I can never get it to answer when I need it to, and the one time I want it to go away, it answers it's fucking self!

Off the bed I go, grabbing the traitorous thing. "H-hello?" I say, waiting to be reamed.

"We're going to pretend you lost service, and your balls didn't just drop, and you're suddenly worried about talking to a female."

"Mommy! My jersey, I need it for volleyball tomorrow." A little girl says in the background.

"I've got it, Iris quit worrying," Winnie says to the child.

"You didn't wash it last week."

"*Once*, child. I forgot *once*. Now, go to bed. Sorry about that, children."

"I remember." I sigh, sitting back on the bed. "Sorry, I panicked-when I heard you talking to the kids."

"Why?" She asks.

"I was breaking in on your routine. I know how hard it is to get one down. I just-I couldn't help but wonder if you were okay. I mean, you had to run off and didn't even say so."

"Yeah, sorry about that. The group I was with Saturday, well, we're all single parents except one, and we all help out. I happen to be the one that gets the bad calls even when it's not my kid. We had one of the fifteen-year-olds decide to get suspended. That's what fights will get you." Her speech is sporadic and even a little labored. She's obviously moving around.

"If it's a bad time, I can let you go. You sound like you got your hands full at the moment."

"Just throwing some clothes in the laundry the joy of preteens deciding they want to wear something that's dirty."

"Winnie, the kitchen is clean. I'm going to sit outside with Lulu." I hear a man's voice, and my heart halts.

"That's fine, Dante. Then you need to finish your work and get a shower because if you can't go to school, you're going to work, and I'm not paying you for it either."

"But-"

"No, buts, you get suspended, you pay. End of discussion."

"Yes, ma'am."

"Speaking of fifteen-year-olds." She laughs, and all the pressure that was building in my chest releases. I can breathe again. For a moment, I was thinking I was going to have to get extra cement.

"So, you all are pretty tight?" I ask, trying to determine the closeness of said friends. I don't mind friends. Hell, I encourage it, but if I'm into somebody, I want them into me. Maybe it's too much to ask, especially when I have the Gabby situation, but why mess with it if I don't have to?

"We see each other every Saturday evening. I see Bryce and Austin the most, but only because I cart their kids to school and pick them up for after school activities. They handle breakfast and lunch. It seems to work for now." She answers honestly as I hear a door, or something shut.

"It must be nice. Having a support system like that. It's always just been my Sofie and me." I lay back on the bed.

"I thank God for them daily. They've been there since before I was married and had kids. I don't think I'd have made it through my divorce without them." She says, getting quiet for a moment. "So, listen as much as I like that you called and sorted yourself out. It's about to get even more awkward than it did earlier. I need to shower, and I don't think I should be putting you on speakerphone to do that."

"How about a bath then? It's been a while since I stretched out in my tub." A smile plays at my lips. "You could grab a glass of wine, and we could just chat."

"And take a bath together? Is that your way of getting me naked?"

"What's good for the goose, I suppose. It is only fair. I mean, you were straddled across my bare back today."

"I was giving you a massage! It's part of my job. I could have let one of the guys do it."

"No need to get defensive. It was very nice. I would very much like to return the favor in the none too distant future." My voice muffles as I pull off my shirt. I'm on the edge of the bed. I lift the phone and take a selfie of just my bare chest and abs before hitting send. "So, how's about it?"

"I'm not defensive. I was just saying-one second." I hear her suck in air. "I didn't make you strip this time. Yeah, okay."

Chapter 9- Winnie

"So, tell me, is this something you do often? Call women, hang up on them, and then ask them to take a bath with you?" I ask Jarrett after finally settling into the bath.

I hear the water shift and clacking. "Actually, no. This is my first shared bath." Before I can say anything, the phone chirps, and it's the alert for video.

You can't be serious! Thank God for bubbles. Wonder bras can be amazing. I hit the accept button on the phone and hold my breath waiting for the video to come up. There he is, laying most comfortably in a big tub, filled like mine with bubbles. I can see the steam coming off him as he smiles at me. Ginger did a good job, took him from Grizzly Adams to just this side of fuck me now, Sir.

"Looks like Ginger done a great job with you," I say, biting my bottom lip.

"I'm told it was all to your direction, so thank you." He holds his squared jaw in his hand and turns his face left then, right. The edges are clean and precise. Not quite as sharp as I'd have done, but close.

"I just told her to do something I thought would work for your face. How do you like it?"

"It works. It shouldn't be hard to maintain." He looks at me. "Are you gonna hold me like that all night or prop me up on something to free up your hands?" He raises a brow.

"I need free hands. Why do I need free hands?" I question as I prop him up on the wooden table that goes over my tub.

"I dunno, maybe you're gonna wanna wash your hair. I mean, a good scrubbing is part of the bathing ritual, is it not?" He holds up a loofah and a bottle of Dove moisture-rich for men.

"Yeah, but in the shower. I'm not washing my hair in the bubbles. It will kill it." I look at him like he's crazy.

"Hmm, then I guess you get to talk to me while I scrub a dub dub." He smirks, and his eyes light up with mischief.

"Tubs are meant for soaking and relaxing. I didn't even have one except in the kid's bathroom until three years ago."

"That how long the Mister's been out of the picture?" He asks, soaping up. I swear he's teasing to get back for the tension during his massage.

RESOLUTION

"Um-" I say, distracted from watching him. "That's how long we've been divorced. He's been gone longer than that. Can't really be there when you're sleeping with fresh out of school nurses." I say, snapping out of it.

He shakes his head as water pours down over his arms, chest, and stomach. Lord, please let the bubbles part like the red sea. "I'm sorry. Gabby, that's Sofia's mom. She beat it when Sofie was four months old. I didn't much see her after that. Not for a long time."

"Brad hasn't seen the kids in over a year. I think Ivy said he was having a kid with his girlfriend. Not that he'll help the poor girl take care of it, but that's life. I just hope she's got a support team."

"Ivy? That's your daughter, and Crew is your son? You also have Iris, correct?" He watches me sitting up a bit more in the tub.

"Crew is my oldest. He'll be thirteen in March. Ivy and Iris-" I pause for a moment. I'm going to say this, and he's going to hang up and disappear, but there is no getting past it, I have twins. "They'll be ten this summer, already planning their summer party."

"Twin girls? *That*... Has to be eventful on a daily basis." He chuckles. "Nine. I remember nine. Thinking they're gonna start with the makeup and the shorter skirts *without* tights. Hairspray and ugh! The glitter parade."

Or maybe not? "They have the girlie down trust me, but they also do band, volleyball, martial arts, and lacrosse, so I like to think they are well rounded."

"Have you built the hobby room yet? I can give you pointers, or better yet, I've got a ton of stuff I can part with." He reaches forward, and everything goes black. I hear the water swooshing, and a moment later, light returns, and we're on the move. "So much stuff. I tell ya." He says breathlessly.

"Hobby room is going to have to wait in this house. We're kind of full in the inn."

He chuckles and enters a room from the sounds of it. A light flips on, and he reverses the camera—my God. I thought I was an organization queen! The man has got three walls of shelves, bins, and totes, color-coordinated, and *sized*! Tables for cutting, crafting, and a sewing station. "Sofie fancied herself a little bit of a diva, dance recitals, and theater projects meant I had to step up my daddy game."

"Piper, one of my best friends, she did all that crazy. I can do hair, nails, makeup, even massages but not that crafty stuff. I suppose you can say it's my shortcoming."

He turns the phone back, and from the low angle, all I get is a happy trail and towel for a second. "Er-sorry. The face is up here." He laughs. "I suppose we all have something we just can't do, me? It's staying awake in a movie theater longer than two hours. Anything over that and the dark environment just knocks me right out."

"You're doing better than me. I took Crew for his first date just after Christmas and fell asleep in the back row. Needless to say, he wasn't happy with me."

"Why? Do you snore like a dragon? Because that's a deal-breaker. I can't be ribbing you in the night just to get my forty winks in." The smirk he's got makes me want to eat his face.

"Worse, actually. I talk in my sleep. Brad hated it. We even slept in different rooms because of it."

"Well, that all depends on what you got to say. I mean, are you forecasting the weather? Making outlandish predictions about the State of the Union? You know shit, I can pop up on YouTube and get us paid for? Or are you going to be just calling out random fantastical things? My name, for instance?"

I clear my throat turning off the camera for a second to get out of the tub, dry off, and put my robe on. "You know you're much more cocky over video than in person." I finish turning the video back on and setting up the phone on the sink to start removing makeup.

"A man is often cockier when his cock is not on the block." Jarrett sighs. "Truth? It's been a long time since I've really just talked to anybody. I mean, I got the couple of guys I work with, but mostly I keep to myself. I don't have a group. Not like you have."

"I wouldn't take you for a loner. I mean, you talked to me that first day at the doctor. Now, look where we are. We're taking baths together, one of us massaged the other, and one of us got hung up on like a teen girl. Oh-You know nothing too weird about that." Shew, I came close to saying something about seeing his face while fucking another man. That wouldn't have been good.

"You're cute when you ramble."

"I don't ramble." I shake my head, climbing onto the bed.

"So is that where we're headed now? The bed?" He asks, turning the phone to face him. It's king-size with a padded headboard; actually, it looks like the whole wall behind the bed is padded. Perhaps soundproofed?

"You can go anywhere you want. I just figured comfort was best. For me to get comfortable someplace other than my bed would wake at least one kid up, so the bed it is."

The phone and presumably him flies through the air and bounces on the bed. "Bed is good, but tell me, Miss McCormick, now that you've got me here, what do you plan to *do* with me?"

I can think of a few things I can do *to* you, but you're not here. "Um, I don't frankly know. I haven't really ever video chatted with anyone. Especially while I'm in the bath or the bed."

"You don't know? Or you won't *say*?" He leans back, and I get a nice long shot of stomach to face. Christ, is he only under his sheet?

"I-I don't know. Well, I *know*, but well, we're still getting to know each other, so those thoughts wouldn't be appropriate." I say in a rush.

"Red's a good color on you. It really makes your eyes pop. I'll tell ya what. I'll show you mine if you show me yours, and tomorrow when we meet for lunch, I promise to kiss you stupid before letting you leave."

"Is this some sort of test?" I ask with a quirked brow. Don't get me wrong. I could get B.O.B. and really show him mine, but why do I feel like doing that would be the wrong thing?

Chapter 10- Jarrett

"Is this some kind of test?" She asks me. Only if she fails. No. Not a test, more of a question of passion plays. Here we are, all alone. Two adults. Why not unwind together after a long, hot, hard day?

"No, Winnie, it's not a test, and if I overstepped, I do apologize, but something tells me you wanna play. At least a little bit. There's a part of you, that lip-biting vixen who is just *dying* to share a good show."

"It's just nothing I've ever done before." She answers almost innocently.

"Then, it'll be a fun first for us both."

"Yeah, really starting to think I pegged you wrong." She says, straightening up. "Toys or no toys?"

RESOLUTION

"The world is your oyster," I answer confidently. Holy shit. This woman is gonna make me lose my ever-loving mind. *Toys?* For fuck's sake. Gabby just likes to gag me and ride me till I blow. This one may make me work for it, and that's fine by me. Give me a chance to dust off my tongue.

"Be right back." She says, flipping the phone, so all I see is the ceiling and her light that's not even on. She must be using the lamp beside the bed because it's bright in there. Did I just hear a lock flick? Jesus Christ. Are we really gonna? With video? What have I started? I'm half-mast at the thoughts running through my head. I put her-er the phone down and roll over, going into my dresser. I'm not making a mess of my nice clean bed. I look, hoping I still have some condoms. I don't use them except for times like these. Well, not *exactly* like these, but you get my drift. Finding one, I set it beside me. Stroking my cock, I pick the phone back up to find her just sitting back down but messing around. Trying to get some music going, it would seem.

"Sorry about that, can't ever be too cautious." She says, just as the song *Damn, I wish I was your Lover* starts. "Damnit, stupid thing. Guess whatever plays is what plays. I can't promise what it will be."

"It works." I smile, licking my lips as my cock goes from half to full sail steel rod. "I did say I'd show you mine. You ready?" I ask with a slight moan.

She pulls her lip into her mouth before nodding and untying her robe. She's got me set up so I can see her whole body. Toes are exactly what I expected. They match her pretty pink nails. "You first."

"Just a second." I grab a few of my smaller pillows, and making a cradle for my phone, set her up so she's got an upshot angle of me. But not, so she's staring at my balls. It's angled high enough that she's looking down on me. I take a deep breath and pull away the remaining bit of the sheet that was covering me. My cock bounces up, aligning itself with my bellybutton.

Her eyes roam over me as she opens her robe. Her legs are crossed demurely, but that doesn't keep me from seeing that she makes use of her waxing facilities. Fresh and clean, just waiting for hardwood. Her creamy skin is flushed from the reveal, and my heart skips beats when I see that each nipple is caged by a ring. A ring that resembles a thumb and forefinger squeezing said nipple to hard perfect points. For a woman that's had three babies, her body is toned, and even the doctor who did her C-section was kind as they cut her below the bikini line.

"You're perfect," I say easily and without any hesitation.

She casts her eyes down but only for a moment. "You're not so bad yourself. At least my thoughts didn't do me wrong."

"*Thoughts*? Elaborate, better, *demonstrate*." I say, stroking the tip of my cock, she watches me a moment, and I see her chest heave as she reaches for something off-camera. A few seconds

RESOLUTION

later, I hear a low humming sound, and in her hand is a pink vibrator, one of those ones that have large round heads. She starts by tickling a nipple, teasing it to attention. I'm sure that the tight nub of flesh stretches through the piercing. She lets out a little moan as she lets the thing run down her breast and her flat stomach. She lifts her knees, obscuring my view for a moment. The anticipation is such a turn on. Slowly she opens her legs, revealing bare lips. With one hand, she opens herself up, letting me see her swelling clit and perfect pink slit. Winnie rubs her clit a bit before slipping her middle finger inside herself. With a moan, her back arches, and her ass lifts off the bed. The vibrator is on her clit, and I'm pulled in. Watching it assault her tender flesh. Her moaning gets louder, breathing more rapid. Holding herself open, I watch as her cum works its way down to the crack of her ass. I stroke faster, imagining my tongue lapping up every drop she gives like a man dying of thirst, finding himself in a sudden rainstorm.

I feel the building need in my balls. The pit of my stomach does somersaults, and precum oozes, making a slippery situation. I get that condom on so I can thrust harder into my tightened fist. Winnie turns the vibrator over, guiding the pulsing thing into her deep wet hole. Now she's tweaking her breast, moaning, and fucking herself exquisitely. She's a woman who knows what she wants and just how to get there. I can't hold back anymore.

"Winnie, don't stop, but I'm gonna come." I grit out, and her crystal blue eyes connect with mine. A devilish smile works across her face as she flicks her tongue at me. I'm a goner, cum erupts, filling the tight condom at an alarming rate. My heart is pounding as I watch her pull the vibrator from between her legs.

"Goon-night, Jarrett." She smiles, leaning toward the phone.

"Wait, no. You don't have to go." I say hurriedly.

"I'll see you at one." The video goes black, and I'm alone to clean up the mess. My head hits the pillow. What a woman.

Chapter 11- Winnie

I left Dante at the salon. I needed to talk to someone that has never judged me on anything before meeting Jarrett for lunch. I've just parked outside Sweet'ums. Brent's inside as he always is, and he better not be fucking one of the waitresses in the office. Walking in, people are everywhere, getting ready for the lunch rush.

I stop seeing Brett, one of the hosts. "Hey, where's Brent?"

"He should be in his office, but it's about the time he takes a break."

"Ah, gotcha." Back out, I go and around the lot. There he is, with smoke surrounding him. "Hey, you," I call out.

Leaned casually against the brick wall of the building, he turns his head, looking at me. Coffee in one hand, vape in the other. "Hey, Chiquita, where you off to looking too cute?"

I may have changed from work clothes to date clothes-striped shorts, maroon tee-shirt, and wedges.

"I have a date with Jarrett Brooks," I say, trying to sound casual.

"Hence the look of nervousness." He turns the vape toward me. "You're gonna need this more than me."

"Stop it," I say, smacking his hand away. "I needed a sounding board because I may have done something last night that I shouldn't have done."

He crooks a brow and flashes a toothy grin. "Did you now?" He sucks down another drag blowing the smoke into my face. "Do tell."

"Dick!" I growl at him. "Anyways, so he came into the Salon-"

"Oh, I heard. Clara decided to cut out after sixth, was gonna have you do her brows, but saw you and Jarrett heading toward the back. She said he was, and I quote, *watchin' dat ass sway*." More smoke in my face.

"I swear I'm going to make her go back to kindergarten if she doesn't start talking right. Ivy has picked up that shit from her. He wanted a massage, asked for me, and I was free. You've had a massage from me." I clear my throat, trying to gather my words. "Only with his the tension was so thick you'd have to cut it with a chainsaw. I had just finished his wash when I got the call about Dante. We had already decided to meet today, but then he called me last night, and we sort of took a bath together."

RESOLUTION

He chuckles an- "Uh-huh. How do you sorta take a bath with a man, *not* in your home? Or did he come over?"

"We were talking on the phone, and I was going to hang up, but he mentioned taking a bath, so instead, he got in his tub and me in mine. Then he turned the video on." I say, biting my lip.

"Well, if that isn't upping the ante. So I'm to assume you're not freaking out over a little bubble spillage. I'm getting a strong porno vibe." If the man ever had a straight face, you would never know it by the riotous laughter he's trying desperately to conceal.

"He pulled the *I'll show you mine if you show me yours*. So I asked, toys or no toys. Did I completely fuck up?"

He chokes on his smoke. "What did you use? Not the double penetrator I got you for your birthday?" He looks horrified.

"No, I used the duel wand. Just tell me if I should just not go on this date. If I should disappear."

"Well, how was he after?" Brent asks, watching me closely.

"He finished, and I hung up on him."

He facepalms. "Any contact since?"

"No." I barely get the word out when my phone dings in my pocket. "Great, what now?"

JARRETT: How are my edges? See you soon.

Incoming attachment: It's a picture of his smiling face. He does have a pretty smile. You can see the salt and pepper look coming in. I have a thing for that look. I've always loved Sam Elliot in Roadhouse because of this look.

"So, I would be wrong," I say, turning the phone for Brent to see.

"Looks like he showered for the occasion. That's *something*."

"How upset is Bryce going to be?" I ask while typing out a message to Jarrett.

WINNIE: Looks good. Don't be late.

"This is Bryce. He's got too much going on to let it really faze him. So long as you all dating don't fuck up the routines, he' isn't gonna want anything more than you happy. Least, that's what I'm going to encourage him to feel." His vape has gone dry. "Seems I'm done. Now you need to run along. Where you meeting him?"

"Kirby's Krab shack?"

"Ahh. That should be fun." He kisses my cheek and opens the fire exit door. "Call me later?"

"Yeah, I'll call you. Man, I really need a smoke now." I say with a wave.

It doesn't take me long to get to the restaurant. I really hope that Jarrett is already here because I'm suddenly starving. Snatching my purse from the passenger seat, I get out and head inside. I spot Jarrett sitting outside by the water as I'm walking toward the door. He stands as I walk toward him. He's in a nice pair of jeans and a t-shirt.

"Hey, I hope you haven't been waiting long," I say, stopping beside him. I reach up and kiss his cheek.

"A few minutes, but I'm working just up the way." He says his hand on my hip as I kiss him. He breaks away and pulls out the chair beside him. "Please sit."

Not across from him like most would but beside him. Hmm? I take my seat and place my purse in the chair beside me. "Do you come here often?"

"I've been here a few times, it's convenient, and the food is really good. Plus ocean views." He points behind him. "I've been working on this place for like eight months now."

"What is it you do *exactly*? If you're working on a place, I'm to assume it isn't real estate, which is what I thought from the card you handed me."

"Basically, it's real estate. Only I'm my own broker. No middlemen. I buy rundown and foreclosed properties, fix them, renovate, and sell them on the open market. Typically for at least twice if not three or four times what I paid for them. It's fun, really. Getting a new place and imagining what I can do to it. Some I've stripped to their bones. Others, it's just tweaks. This place, though. It's going to be perfect for someone with a family. If I had other kids, I'd be keeping it, hands down." He sounds so excited and is animated as he talks.

"Is that something you want? More kids?" I ask. I figure it's something we should know now rather than later.

He looks at me. "I don't know. I mean, I'm not *opposed* to the idea. I love being a daddy. It's the best thing in this world, but Sofie is all grown up now. There are only so many things left to teach her. I'm still young enough to enjoy little ones, be they mine or not, doesn't make much difference to me." He leans closer to me. "What about *you*? I mean, are kids a deal-breaker?"

"Not a deal-breaker, just I hadn't planned to have anymore. With an almost thirteen-year-old boy and two almost ten-year-old girls, it's already hectic. With my age, the chances that I would have another multiple birth, well, let's just say two or more, could happen. I barely handled the two together."

"I can see where that could be something to give you pause. I mean if the pregnancy was difficult-" He stops looking up. A server comes over with a tray. "I totally spaced. I ordered a few things to get us started. I wasn't sure how long you would have."

"I've got time. Piper and I traded cars, so she's picking up the kids today. I was supposed to be with Dante at the salon, but I gave him a list that should be done by the time I get back." I smile at him. "As for pregnancy- with Crew, it was a breeze. The girls came almost three months early."

"Christ." His hand covers mine. "Sofie was a preemie too. Came at thirty weeks. Gabby was in a car accident, and it sent her into labor. I almost lost them both. You must have been out of your mind."

RESOLUTION

I try not to laugh but can't stop myself. "Brad wasn't there, actually. He was off on a business trip—some kind of conference or something. The group of friends I told you about, we do holidays together or try to. We were having our annual Independence Day cookout when my water broke. I hadn't even hit thirty weeks yet. Brent and Piper stayed with me day and night as we fought to try and keep longer. They decided by the seventh they were done, and I was officially thirty weeks that day. They weighed a pound and three ounces each. We were in the hospital for a while."

He nods. "I remember them telling me Sofie's lungs were underdeveloped, and she was so yellow. She had jaundice because her liver was rejecting Gabby's blood type. We didn't do typing. No one thought to mention it to us. But A and O are not exactly compatible. Her little body decided it wanted to be A, like her daddy, and it made her sick. I was beside myself for two days before they figured it out."

"I would have been so scared. I would have never thought to do blood typing either." I shake my head, not sure what to say. I look at the food around us. "Did you order everything?"

"Um-I wasn't sure if you were one of those carbs are the enemy types or not, so I ordered a little of this and a little of that." There's that wide full smile again.

"I wouldn't be able to keep up with all the kids if it weren't for carbs. I quit watching my figure years ago. I figure as long as I love my body. That is all that matters."

Chapter 12- Jarrett

Fuck. She smells fantastic. Looks great, even with a Kirby's Krab Shack bib covering two of her best assets. Winnie's got an appetite, that's for sure. We murdered the samples I ordered, including the loaf of bread with butter to dip. I'm relieved to find a woman so comfortable in her skin. Confidence is the sexiest trait any woman can possess. It doesn't matter if she's a size four or thirty-four. If she carries herself with her head high and a great attitude, she's the hottest woman in the room. Right now, Winnie is working on her drink, and I've never wanted to be a straw so bad in my life.

She looks up at me through long dark lashes. "What? Why are you looking at me like that?"

"I was just thinking, how that straw has the best job in the world right now," I say it before my brain can stop me.

"Tell me how you really feel."

"I feel like kissing you." I grasp her chair, turning her toward me.

"Um, here?"

"Why not? It's a beautiful day, the sun is shining, and I promised to kiss you stupid if we had that bath. You came through, so now it's my turn." Taking the fork from her hand, I place it on the plate before pulling her into my personal space. Her body is a little tight as she watches me, with a lick of her lips. That's all the encouragement I need. My hands go to the sides of her face, and I cup her cheeks as I let my lips touch hers. I can feel the breath she's holding as I kiss again, my lips teasing hers apart just a fraction. I change my angle and kiss her a third time; now I seek to part her lips entirely, and as I do, her hands go to my upper knees, and she breathes into me, finally kissing me back.

Her hands grip the sides of my shirt as her tongue rubs against mine. My mind races, and my thoughts go back to last night. Images flashing, her naked on the bed. Those nipple rings, I wonder if she's wearing the same ones today. I growl just a little. All I want to do right now is take this woman someplace and fuck her till she can't walk. I need to calm my ass down. Winnie isn't some seventeen-year-old girl. You can just fuck in the back of your truck. Do you really just want another aimless notch in the bedpost, or do you want to explore the possibility of something more substantial? I pull back, breaking the kiss, and I swear the kick to my balls is my cock calling me a pussy.

She clears her throat. "Just a few more minutes, and I probably would have come from never being kissed quite like that."

"I could finish you off if you like *after* I pay the check." Cock is trying to control the mouth.

"As much as I'd love nothing more, I think it may be too soon for that."

"No, I agree. I just meant that I'm prepared to spend a little time in the back seat of my truck making out with you if you are game." I smile, wiping a bit of smudged lipstick off the side of her mouth.

"So, we're teenagers again?"

"I'd take you to the house I'm working on, but it's not furnished yet. Except for a couple of benches made out of beams and buckets. The truck is more comfortable than that."

"You can fit in the backseat of a truck?"

"For our purposes, yes, and it's a large truck. I'm figuring it will keep us... *Controlled*." I lean into her. "See, if I had it my way, you'd be naked with your arms around my neck while I pound you senseless, but I think we need at least three dates before *that* can happen."

"Let me get this straight, you're fine with me straddling you to give you a massage, you're fine being on video while we're both in the bath, even more so watching me come, but it takes three dates to fuck me stupid? Which I'm inclined to agree with. I'm just trying to figure out your logic."

"Forgive me for being scattered brained," I say, my hand on her soft, supple thigh. "I've got two heads, and they're in direct opposition while dueling it out for dominance as we speak. I know that the right thing to do is wait, get to know you more deeply, but my cock is saying I can learn a lot more by being balls deep in you on the marble floor of my six-bedroom beach house estate. Which, if we pay right now, could happen in about twelve minutes."

Winnie bites her lip, watching me. "I should say no. The right thing would be to stay here and get to know one another better. At the same time, we shouldn't have let last night happen either. There's something about you that makes me giddy and wants to see what else you've got."

My hand squeezes her thigh, and I kiss her again for just a moment as I grab the check. "Let's go."

Paid and hornier than the devil, I lead her to the parking lot. "Do you wanna follow me, or do you want me to drive?" I point at my truck.

"I'd better follow. Piper would kill me for leaving her baby." She points to where she's parked. I'm looking at an emerald green mustang with a metallic fleck.

"Guess your friend is doing pretty well," I say as she turns toward it. I walk her to it. I don't want to let her out of my sight. I don't want her to lose her nerve. Or maybe it's me who I'm afraid will come down from this high? We get to the mustang, and I pin her to it. Grasping her by the

RESOLUTION

ass and lifting her to my six foot three height, I assault her mouth again.

"Follow me to my place at least that way, we'll have comfort. Better yet, get your phone out." She pulls out her phone, and the next thing I know, mine is ringing with video. "You like video so much. Let's see how long you last."

My jaw twitches. "Get in the car. I'm right behind you."

"That's the plan." She says as I put her down. She bends, putting her stuff in so her ass is facing me. In those little shorts, all I wanna do is slip them aside, part her thighs and taste her.

Just one good swipe. I'm sure she's wet by now. I sidle up behind her and get it, so my body blocks one angle and the car the other. She tries to straighten up, but I press her down with one hand as the other inches up her thigh. Her breath hitches when my other fingers round her tight little ass. Winnie is half squatting, a perfect angle to let my fingers do the talking. I slip her shorts, and with them, her panties aside, jackpot, her pussy is hot and slick, just aching to be licked, pulled, teased, all in preparation for riding my fat hard cock. I curl my middle and ring finger up and down her slit. Her hands go flat, and her back end raises more as I dip into her tight little pussy. I get to the second knuckle and stroke her like a kitten.

With a low moan, she drops her head, and her knees begin to bend. I grab her center, pulling her against me, speeding up my fingerbang. Her pussy clenches and her breathing intensifies as I feel her come. Once she thoroughly drenches my fingers, I slide them from her and help her to sit in the mustang. I suck her cum from my fingers.

"Christ, you taste like clover, honey." I smile. "I can't wait to bury my tongue inside you next."

Chapter 13- Winnie

Fuck me running; he actually has balls. After kissing me again and shutting my door, Jarrett damn near runs to his truck. I get my phone set up on the dash to where we can see each other. I figure if we're gonna play, we should *really* play. See, I've started carrying lollipops to help with the cravings. Considering I'm really craving a smoke about now, and I don't feel like chewing on gum. Lollipop it is.

I start the car up as Jarrett gets himself situated. "All good over there?" I ask with a smirk.

"I'm all set." He licks his lips, no doubt still tasting me on them.

We talk back and forth until we hit the first red light then I pull the loli out of my purse. I pull the plastic off and wet my lips before flicking my tongue against the loli.

"Winnie-you're killing me." I hear him grit out. "If I have an accident because my cock rips from my jeans and hits the steering wheel, I promise as soon as I recover, you're gonna need a wheelchair."

"Promises, promises," I say, letting my hand wander up the inside of my shirt. I let out a hiss as I pinch my nipple between my fingers. Today I have lip nipple rings in. Did I mention the windows in this thing are tinted? I glance down, and the look on his face is pure exquisite pain. I look in the rearview, and he's right on my ass.

"You need to drive faster or pull the fuck over."

"It's just a little foreplay," I say, licking the loli again. "Aren't you going to play with me, Jarrett?"

"H-How would you like me to do that and not wind up going over the rails and falling to my death? These curves are almost as dangerous as yours." He glances back down at me and groans. "Look, there's a Marriott coming up. Let's just stop. I can't wait to get my hands on you."

Tsk Tsk. "You don't want to see what other toys I may have?"

He shifts in his seat and facepalms. "Will we be using them?"

"Only if you're a good boy."

"How much further?" He watches as I twist and pull my nipple, further exposing both breasts.

RESOLUTION

"Just a little further. You know I'm betting nobody could see in your truck. You could always pop your fly and play a little too."

"Son of a—" I swear I can hear him grind his teeth. His hand appears over the phone, and his truck slows down a smidge. The phone angle is now *cockeyed*. I watch as he unzips his fly and battles to get his cock from his wranglers. It just misses the steering column as he leans back. "I've hit the cruise control. Let me know if we are gonna hit another section of turns."

"You're good until we turn down my street. Tell me, do I get to lick you the way I am this loli?"

"Absolutely, so long as you don't mind doing it while riding my face." He strokes his cock with his thumb, paying careful attention to the thick pulsing vein on the underside.

"God, I'm so wet. I could probably get off on just thinking about your fingers slipping in and out of me. Hard and fast."

"That's just primer wait until I'm pounding you with eleven inches of hard cock while tapping that clit till you see stars."

"What no ass play? Are you not an ass man?"

The truck swerves. *"Christ."* He looks at me as I suck the whole loli into my mouth with a grin. "You are a woman that knows what she likes, aren't you? If you want me to do something, just ask, and baby, I'm ready to make it happen."

"I have toys for that too. Not everyone is into that, though. We're getting ready to turn off." I say, flicking on my right turn signal.

With a lick of his lips, he grabs the wheel again and follows me. The phone is again accosted and righted as I am to assume are his pants. "How long will we have?"

"Until I decide to go get the kids from Piper. Afraid you're gonna pop too quickly and need to go again?" I ask. "Left here," I say, getting ready to pull in my drive. "Fuck."

"What?" He asks, pulling in right behind me. "Winnie? Are you alright? Who's this clown?"

"Someone who only shows up when he wants to show off his own children. So, uh, never. I'm sorry. I had no idea he'd be here." I put the car in park. Righting myself. I watch in horror as Jarrett exits the truck, looking as pulled together and perfect as when I arrived this afternoon.

Brad's eyes sail from the mustang's front to its side, where Jarrett has stopped. Lord, kill me now! I open the car door after I'm pulled together.

"Who is this, and where's your car?" Brad asks, walking our way. Jarrett angles himself in front of me.

"That's really none of your business," I respond, patting Jarrett's arm.

"Why aren't you at work?"

"That's some more of your business?"

"I want to take the kids this weekend," Brad says, stopping in front of us.

"They have activities, *Brad*. You know you're supposed to call at least a week ahead of time."

"I'll just go get them from school."

"You can't. Please just leave." I say, losing my patience.

RESOLUTION

"I will when *he* does. Why are you running around with my wife anyway?" Brad stands up taller, still not at big as Jarrett.

"Stop it. We're divorced and have been for three years."

"As long as I'm paying for you, you're mine."

"You need to step back," Jarrett says, looking down at Brad. "She's asked you to leave, which means you are now trespassing."

"I pay for this place. I can be here if I want." Brad tries to step closer.

"Damnit, Brad, I'm not doing this with you. I swear to God you only come around when I'm trying to talk to someone."

"I've heard you've done more than talk."

"I'm a big girl; I can do what I want."

"My wife shouldn't be fucking other guys."

"I'm sorry, he's not going to stop. He's delusional, and it's only going to get worse before it gets better. Can I call you later?" I speak to Jarrett because until he leaves, Brad isn't going to stop.

"She's not your *wife*, and that money? When you pay is for your *children*. As I understand, the house has nothing to do with you." Jarrett pulls out his phone. "Now you can kindly get back in your car and vacate the premises, or I can gladly have you forcibly removed. Unless, of course, you'd like to have a go? I'll be happy to put you in your car myself." His voice is calm and cool, as if he were talking to a child.

Brad laughs. "I pay her almost seven thousand a month. She's mine until I decide she isn't." He finishes trying to pull me to him.

Jarrett grabs Brad by the arm, twisting it behind his back. "Touching is a no-no. That's attempted assault." He leans into Brad, who struggles like a bull with a rider. Jarrett whispers something I can't hear, but it's enough to make Brad lash out, clawing the side of Jarrett's face. "Thank you for that." Jarrett smiles, and Brad calls out in agony as he's led to his car.

I lean against the car as Jarrett walks back to me. "I'm so sorry." I'm embarrassed, so I'm not even looking at him.

He tilts my face by the chin, making me look up at him. "Don't you dare apologize for that piece of shit. I'm sorry that I had to be all Alpha male, but I won't have anybody talk to a woman like that in my presence." He breaks eye contact long enough to watch Brad drive away. "Now, why don't we go inside, I'll make you a cup of tea, and you can curl up and watch something on TV?" He leans down and kisses me softly. "I'll take a raincheck for now, but perhaps we can do lunch again? Or maybe dinner? Sofie could come here, keep tabs on the kids, and you could come to my place for dinner. That is if you want to?"

"I can't believe you're even still here. Why are you?"

"I raised a little girl all alone and taught myself to sew like a professional costumer just so she would always smile. What can I say, except I like a challenge."

RESOLUTION

"Guess he kind of ruined everything. I like you, so of course, I'd go out with you again and hope for a better outcome than this."

Chapter 14- Jarrett

Bam! I hit another baseball as it's hurled at me. The batting cages on the boardwalk are a great way to disperse pent up frustrations. I could have broken Brad's fucking arm, but then I'd have had to explain myself to the police officer that would have soon followed. I was true to my suggestion, bringing Winnie into the house, I made her some tea while she changed into some yoga pants and an oversized tee shirt. Once she was settled, I kissed her goodbye with plans to talk later via video chat. She is by far the most fascinating woman, and I am eager to learn more about her and her life. That ex of hers, though, something is going to need to be done about him, that's for sure. If I hadn't been there, just what would he have done? Forced her to do? Thinks because he drives a Ferrari that he's got a big dick to swing. I'll show him a big dick, make him cry for it, too, when I smack him upside his little pinhead with it.

I'm not sure how long I've been in the pen when I hear my phone ring. I turn back and grab it.5241

The machine still throwing fastballs.

"Yeah?"

"Daddy?"

"Sofia, What's wrong?"

"I'm hungry, and you left me home with no car!" She whines.

"Little girl, there's a fridge full of groceries. Eat something."

"I want a double quarter pounder with cheese and bacon, no onions, extra pickles, and honey mustard. I also want curly fries from Arby's and a Frosty. Oh- and can you stop by the grocer and get fudge pops?"

I laugh. "None of that is good for you or the baby."

"Daddy! Please! It's all I want!"

"All you want, you don't say?" I tease. "Alright, I'll be home in about twenty."

"Love you, daddy." She hangs up, and I grab my things, heading out of the batting cages.

I make all the requested stops and am home by five-thirty. Sofia is on the couch, her feet propped up. On her chest, curled up, is a tiny little puff of black fur. I stand in my living room, staring at this furball, bags in my hand. Curious as to how it came to be inside my animal-free home.

"Sofia?" I ask in my most curious tone.

My little girl stretches from her fingers to her toes, like when she was a toddler. Her eyes open just as the black floof picks up its head looking at me. "Hi, daddy." She smiles, scratching it between the ears.

"Why is there a cat on you?"

She sits up, cradling the thing to her chest. "It's a kitten, daddy. I found him outside all alone. Somebody ran over his momma."

"Baby, you know how I feel about cats."

"He's an orphan, daddy. You can't just put him out." She cries, clutching this thing to her. "I'm a grown-up. I can take care of Midnight all by myself."

I smack my head. "Midnight? For Christ's sake, you named it already?" I head for the kitchen. "Where's it gonna sleep? What's it gonna eat out of? Use the bathroom?" I ask, knowing full well I've just become a cat owner.

"I ordered everything online after I talked to you. It should be here-" The doorbell rings. Still clutching the animal, she makes a dash for the door as I'm trying to make heads or tails of the food situation.

"You can just put it in here if you don't mind." I can hear my darling daughter talking to and escorting some stranger into my house.

I look up, and it's a young man holding bags of things, a tub of cat litter, and a big bag of cat food is over his shoulder. My daughter watches as he unloads everything. The look on her face tells me I may see an uptick in deliveries. Lord help me, she's not even signed the divorce papers yet.

"Sofia?" I ask, pulling her out of her fog.
"Daddy?"
"Where did you get the money for this?"
"My emergency credit card?" She smiles at me.

***

"I didn't know what else to do but set her and the cat up in her room," I say to Winnie as I watch her apply lotion to her smooth, toned calves.

"She's got you wrapped around her little finger." Winnie smiles over at me.

"Always has," I admit as her hands disappear and reappear from under her robe while she works up her thighs. "Wish I was there. I could give you quite the rubdown."

"Oh, I bet you would." She laughs, but it's not quite the same as it was at lunch.

"You still chewing on what happened this afternoon?" I ask, laying back in the bed.

"Sort of, but he showed back up at dinner. I thought Crew was going to lose his mind. The girls wanted to go with him. So, now they're mad at me for saying no."

"I'm sorry. I know how hard that can be. Gabby took off early but tried to reconnect when Sofia was thirteen. A lot of broken promises, forgotten calls, missed visits. She was always full of excuses and always forgiven. Let me say or do one thing out of line, though, and she would flip her shit on me. Fortunately for me, as sole guardian, I was able to make her stay away. At least until Sofia was eighteen. It was a rough year following it, but it was what was needed. Eventually, she understood, and your little ones will too. It just takes time."

"That's the thing I don't want him to stay away from them. I want him to want to be around them. If he could leave me alone in the process, that would be awesome. Still, eventually, they're all gonna be off to college and starting families of their own. I've got two little girls who are going to want their daddy to walk them down the aisle, and he's too selfish to see that. I've smoked an entire pack in the last five hours."

"Your head must be ready to explode. All that nicotine at once. You're gonna make yourself sick." I say, concerned as she sits at her vanity, robe open just a hair while she puts on her moisturizer.

"I took something for it already. I needed something, and I didn't have anything handy. The thing is, on top of my kids dealing with their crazy-ass dad, I have Dante. He didn't need to see any of that. Brad decided to tell the kids I was bringing a random man home. So, let's add all *those* questions."

"I'm sorry, and I'll understand it if you don't want to keep seeing me if it's just too much right now. It'll suck, but I'll understand it." I watch for her response.

"Oh, shut up. Am I not talking to you right now?"

"How do I know you're not just looking for your chance to tell me to go fuck myself? You wouldn't be the first woman to lull me into a false sense of security just to throw a drink in my face and never return."

Winnie picks up her phone, and we're on the move. "I'm sorry, did I miss something? Did we not have a good time until it got interrupted?" She gives me a look that says, *what the fuck?*

"I'm sorry, I just-I remember how hard it was when Sofia was little. I can't even begin to imagine doing it times three. I want to give you the chance to walk away if that's what you feel you need to do. Before we go any further. As I said, I hope you won't, but I understand if you do. I mean, honestly? If you told me to shimmy my ass up your trellis and slip into your window, I'd tell you I'll see you in fifteen minutes."

"I could see that going over well. My room is at the front of the house. Someone would call the cops before you could get off the ground."

I chuckle. "It'd be worth the risk. Where are you taking me?"

"Into my closet, I need clothes."

"Do *you*? Do you *really*?" I ask sarcastically.

"Yes, I really do. I can't just walk around in a robe. No matter how much you may like seeing it." She rolls her eyes at me.

"One can dream." I smile, listening as she rifles through her closets.

"Are you sure you wouldn't rather have me in this?" Winnie asks, holding a very see-through nightie in front of her *very* naked body.

"Does the um-fur come off? I'd rather not be picking it out of my teeth for the next week." I lick my lips and adjust my rising cock in my pants.

"No to that one then. Hmm-" She disappears for a second only to come back with a purple nightie in front of her. "Is this one more your speed?"

The damn thing would be torn to shreds in seconds if she wore it in front of me. "You plan to give me another show?"

"Do you need another show? Or are you just trying to see my collection?"

"Can't I have both?"

"I can't show you all my kinks yet. Some may scare you away."

"Winnie, I'm a forty-three-year-old man. If I haven't licked, sucked, or fucked it yet, I'm dying to try it, trust me. You're not scaring me away."

Chapter 15- Winnie

I made it to Sweet'ums before anyone. Brent and I needed to catch up because I may have forgotten to call him the other day. I dropped the kids and my car at Austin's before grabbing an uber over here. Walking in, I grab a drink on my way to the office.

"Brenton, if you are fucking a bar slut, I will beat you to death," I yell, coming through the hall. Just as I approach out from his door comes Lexi, one of the hostesses, wiping the side of her mouth. "You should know better," I say as she gives me the stink eye. I lean against the door and see that Brent is still putting himself back together. "It's Saturday! Shouldn't you be, I don't know, getting ready for *us*?"

Looking me straight in the face, he replies. "This *is* how I get ready for you lot. I mean, with how short Piper's skirts are and tight Tatum's pants tend to get, I can't go out there with a loaded gun. That would be suicide. I promised myself no more sad hookups with either of them. It's not fair to any of us."

"Bryce is going to try tonight, but it's not happening. I can't let it, not with the way this week has been. That'd be wrong."

"So you and Mister Brooks had a *very* good time, I assume?" He grins at me, waving me out of his office and toward the fire exit. "Smokie time."

"Lunch was nice. Car ride to my house, even better. Pulling into my driveway, not so much." I say, following along behind with my drink.

"Why, what happened? Wait, let me guess, *Bradly*. Clara said Dante mentioned him just showing up."

"He told the kids I was bringing a random guy home. Dante was there, so I'm sure everyone knows now. I just don't want tonight to be full of drama, ya know?"

"Chiquita, are you having some fun?"

"I am, but maybe I shouldn't be. I should be worrying about the kids more than myself right now. I shouldn't have brought him home. Christ, Brent, what have I done?"

"Nothing bad or wrong. You've been divorced from that sack of shit for three years. Prior to your divorce, that rat bastard was giving it to everybody but you for almost four years, or don't you remember the first vibrator I bought you? Shit, you burned it out in four months! You need dick like most need air. It's why you started sleeping with Bryce in the first place, even if he is a bit vanilla for the new you." He puts his arm around me. "If this guy lets you let your freak flag fly, I'm all for it."

"I'm worried about the kids. The girls won't talk to me. Crew's asking so many questions, and I don't have any answers."

"I find being honest with them is best. If you try and lie and you get caught, they will never forgive it. I think Crew is old enough to understand you wanting to date, and the girls, they still have hopes about their daddy. It won't be easy, but hiding the man isn't gonna be easy or fair either."

"Honestly, Crew just wants to know more about him and to meet him, but I'm not sure if either of us is ready for that. They're all staying at Austin's tonight. I'm supposed to go over and get them after I get my shopping done tomorrow. Crew and Dante have eaten me out of the house. Right now? I really need to get drunk, and you need to keep Bryce from trying to take me home."

"I think I can handle that." Brent takes a long drag from his vape. "You want a little? I won't tell." He turns the pipe over to me.

"I shouldn't. I smoked a whole pack last night and made myself sick." I shake my head.

"It's not *nicotine*." He smirks. "I got in a batch of Merry Cherry Cannabis."

"Oh, so not only are we getting drunk, you want me to be high too? I should just lock away my phone now?" I laugh and take a drag from the vape.

"You afraid you're gonna drunk dial, Mister Brooks?" He watches me. "You should-it would do ya some good."

"That's a possibility, and I'd rather not. Do me good? It could be bad instead of good."

"Ain't nothing bad about letting him get his tip wet if it gets you off too. Come on." He says, looking at his phone. "The rest of the pack has arrived. Tatum just texted me."

"Interrogations here we come," I say, taking one more drag and then downing my drink.

I grab another drink on my way to the table. I drop my purse beside Austin before sitting down. As I let my eyes glance over everyone, I notice Bryce isn't here. Is that my fault? I hope not.

"So, how's the hunk that showed up at the Salon?" Tatum is the first to open her mouth.

"I suppose he's doing well," I say, acting like it doesn't bother me.

"According to Ashton, who heard it from Dante, you got strange men now. I'm guessin' it's something you feel you gotta hide?" Austin smirks, tipping his beer back.

"First, Dante was listening to Brad stirring up shit. So, I took a guy home. What's so wrong with that? The kids weren't home, but Brad was there when we pulled up and decided to put hands on me, and Jarrett wasn't having it. Brad left, then came back after the kids got home saying all kinds of shit. Crew is mostly just asking questions, but the girls won't speak to me." I sigh, dropping my head.

RESOLUTION

Austin gently rubs my back. "You are a woman in need of- Drinks!" He hollers, getting every waitress in the joint's attention. "We need shots! Lots of shots!"

Brent snickers, scrolling over his phone. "Bryce is home tonight, says Echo has that stomach thing that's going around."

"Tell him I'll drop stuff off tomorrow after I hit the store," I say instinctually.

"You know you're going to break Bryce's heart if you're serious about this other guy," Piper says, getting my attention.

"No, I'm not. I don't think there's anything wrong with me talking to someone and making something serious out of it or trying to anyway. I'm still surprised he's even wanting to come around after Brad. By the way, can I borrow your car again, and you do pick up duty on Tuesday?"

"Another date *already*?"

"Yeah, why not?"

"Clara has decided to take up Choir for the second leg of the year, so she's staying after. I'll trade ya. Besides, why drive a mustang when you can drop the top down on my corvette?" Brent says as the first round of kamikaze's is delivered.

"Are you sure you can handle all the kids and everywhere they have to be?" I smile. "You do remember it's three sets of twins; nine, seven, and three, then Crew, right?"

"First of all, I was there for all them births, so yeah, I remember, and secondly, them girls love me. Besides, if Crew is full of questions, who better to lay it out for him than me?"

"No, no, absolutely not! You are not answering any of those questions. I remember when you scared Clara! She was freaked out until I talked her down. He's twelve, not sixteen."

"Right, and maybe if someone had talked to me at twelve, I would have kept it in my pants a bit longer. Instead, I was behind the Starbucks getting my thirteen-year-old pecker sucked by fifteen-year-old Judy Fields and her cousin Martha!"

Austin chokes on his drink. "Seriously? You told me you never had sex with Martha."

"A blow job is not penetration." Brenton chuckles. "I may have been taught by them to lick pussy, but I didn't fuck till Breanne. That was the end of eighth grade."

"Change the subject because I am just not drunk enough to hear this crazy."

Chapter 16- Jarrett

Beep! Beep! Beep! My phone chirps like a truck backing up, alerting me to a message. Rolling over, I look at the clock. It's half past three in the morning. What the fuck? I squint, looking at the blinding white screen.

WINNIE: Attachment:
I'm looking at her pink nipple encased in what looks like a frosted pink cupcake with sprinkles.

JARRETT: Have we been drinking?
WINNIE: Me? Never!
Attachment:
A bottle of Maker's Mark between her thighs. Is she sitting on a bar?

JARETT: Where are you?

Incoming call:
I answer, and she's half laying on what looks to be exactly what I thought. The bar at Sweet'ums. How do I know this? Because the decor is that Muppet for which the place is aptly named. She's got on skinny black jeans and a silky long-sleeved striped blouse, which is unbuttoned to her belly while she plays with her breasts.

"Winnie, they're gonna have to sterilize that counter if you keep at that. Why aren't you at home?"

"I'm waiting on my Uber, then I'll lock up and go home. If I get off right here, we'll keep it as our dirty little secret."

"When did you call the Uber?" I ask, sitting up.

"I don't know–half an hour ago or so."

"You're all alone?" My concern is building.

"Yeah, Brent had a date, so I'm locked in the place waiting. I'm fine. I do this from time to time." Her words are slurred, and from the way my head is starting to spin, I'd say her coordination is suffering.

I get up, tossing on my sneakers, and grab my keys. "Stay put. I'm coming to get you."

"What? No, I'm fine. I just wanted to talk before I went home and crashed."

"So talk to me while I drive. I'm already halfway to the truck."

"Jarrett, I'm *fine*, really. I've just gotten so used to talking to you. I don't usually stay this late."

"If an Uber doesn't show after thirty minutes, it's not coming." I start my truck. "Look, you got two choices, talk to me, and make me feel more at ease over your wellbeing, or hang up and let me go outta my mind with worry. What are you gonna do to me?"

"Lick you like I did the loli on Thursday."

I crack a smile. "As much as I'd like that, unless you let me pick you up, there's no chance of it."

"Tell me, Jarrett, what's one of your fantasies? Something you've thought about but never done?" She lets out a small moan as her hand disappears from her nipple. I can't see what's she's up to, but I have a pretty good idea.

I clear my throat. "A fantasy, huh? I'm up for just about anything, but something that has eluded m?. Something I've craved doing and never done?" Her moans get deeper. Fucking hell. "Sex in a public place. Like be out during the day or even an evening and be with a woman who hikes up her skirt and gets into my lap." I say and feel the bulge start in my pants. Now I'm regretting not putting on jeans and just hurrying out in my sleep pants.

"Sex in a public place. So, with people watching?" Her little moans come again.

"More like with people unaware. Like in a park or at the layout at the drive-in movie. Ya know, my back against a tree, you unzip me and back up on to me, sitting on my cock. Letting me slowly fuck you so that you can feel every stroke as I move. You just lean into me and let me fill you up until you can't take it anymore and come all over me. I think that would be so good. Though the idea of others actually watching might be hot too. Let them see what they're not getting." My cock is hard as a rock as I pull around the corner toward Sweet'ums. "Christ, you've got me going, just talking about this stuff."

"Oh, God, Jarrett, I'm so close."

"I'm here. Let me in." I pull up to the restaurant and kill the lights as I hop out, headed for the doors.

She opens the door with her hand still down her pants while pulling me in and down to her with the other. I relock the door as she attempts to devour my lips in a kiss. Giving over to her, I let our tongues entangle as my hands grab the sides of her pants, giving them a forceful yank. She yips into me when I step into them to free her of them once and for all. Grasping her by the ass, I lift her, walking with her. I open my eyes and, locating the nearest table, I put her down, scattering everything that was on it. Bam goes the ketchup, as does the salt and pepper. Sugar, napkin dispenser. Winnie bites her bottom lip as I tear open her shirt and reveal a sheer underwire bra with little black hearts all over it. I make quick work of the front closure clip.

Her chest heaves, and her hands go into my hair, racking my scalp as I flick her nipple at the center of the ring.

"Christ, Winnie," I whisper. "Can you feel what you do to me?" I pull her down the table,

RESOLUTION

rubbing against her sweet wet folds my pants.

you want me to lick and suck it like I loli?" She asks, licking her lips.

pull her up, kissing her. "Come home with and I promise I'll make you see stars."

"Sofie's there." She says as her hands play with my waistband.

"She had a date, didn't come home, but left me a lovely message." My fingers trail up her thigh. "I just don't want our first encounter on a sticky barroom floor."

She licks her lips, watching me. "Your neighbors are going to get quite a show with me like this."

I pick her up, crushing her against me. "It's a good thing I live in a house surrounded by trees."

Chapter 17- Winnie

"Fuck. Shit. God, Dammit."

I cry as the pain in my head is trying to kill me. It hurts to even open my eyes. I start to crack them open, and I know automatically I'm not in my house. Who the fuck did I go home with? I've got some kind of shirt on, but other than that, I'm naked. Christ! Birth control or not, I need to get the morning-after pill to be on the safe side. There's heat all over my back. I turn over, looking beside me, and all I see is the back of a man's head. Great, just great. I turn to slip from the bed. Where are my clothes? I'm feeling around on the floor, trying to find anything. So far, I'm coming up empty. As I look under the bed, I hear movement, followed by the blanket on the other side lifting.

RESOLUTION

"You looking for an escape hatch?" I'm staring at the upside-down face of Jarrett.

"Clothes?" I ask as innocently as I can muster.

"Still on my front seat. I think. I wasn't really worried about them when I carried you in this morning."

I sit back, wrapping my arms over my chest. "What happened last night? Did we um-have sex? Was I okay?" I ramble.

"You were very drunk when you called me. We talked, you teased. I came to get you because your Uber never showed. We fooled around a little, which led to your current clothing situation, but no, we didn't have sex. Mostly it was kissing, then you crashed in the truck, so I brought you up here and put you to bed."

"I'm so sorry. I don't usually get like that."

"After the week you've had, I'm surprised I wasn't picking you up off the floor sooner." He pats the bed beside him.

I climb up and into the bed but sit sort of away from him. "Brent may have been pumping me full of his cannabis oil vape, and it was mixed with drinks."

"Hmm." He grabs me and pulls me to him. Christ, he's got long arms. "Good morning." He smiles.

"Morning," I say, watching him. Playing over the phone and in public is much different than being alone with someone in a bed.

"How often do you get to start your day with an orgasm?" Jarrett's hands trace down to my hips. "I promised I was going to make you see stars."

"Um-well, never. Did you?" I ask as I get flutters in my belly.

"I thought best to leave it until you would remember it. Like, say now." His hands grasp me, and the next thing I know, I'm on my back, lengthwise across his giant bed.

"Jarrett, Sofie?" I ask breathlessly.

"Isn't home, and if she is, the room is soundproofed. Feel free to moan my name repeatedly. If you like." He parts my thighs and pressing down on my stomach; I feel his tongue connect with my clit.

***

Jarrett pulled into my drive so I can clean up before going to get my car when my phone rings. Without looking, I answer it.

"Hello?"

"Chiquita, what did you do in my bar?" Brenton's voice comes through, and boy, does he ever sound mad.

My eyes dart to Jarrett's. "I'd love to answer that, but I can't. I don't really remember anything. I love you," I say with a cringe.

"Yeah? You *love* me? Love shoulda kept my ketchup bottle intact last night. Just tell me you all didn't do nothing kinky with it before you broke it."

"Again, I don't think so. This is all your fault. You know I don't mix well."

"You owe me, if ya got any, you *really* owe me."

"Does tongue count?"

"Aye! Chiquita. Would you ride that stallion already! You've got an empty house and a fine chest of toys. Go utilize them!" He hangs up on me. A second later, a text comes through with six eggplant emoji and a peach.

Getting out of the truck, I come around to Jarrett. "We um didn't do anything with a ketchup bottle, right?"

He squints at me. "That's a little above my pay grade. We may have cleared a table with your body, though."

"Okay. Do you want to come in?" I ask, heading for the door.

"Sure." He follows behind me, two steps, and I can feel him beside me.

Open the door; I let him go in before so I can lock it behind. With Brad lurking around, you never know. "So, I apparently owe Brent. No idea what kind of mess I or we made, but I owe him."

"You blew through a bottle of Maker's Mark and may or may not have come all over his bar," Jarrett says, turning to face me. "Frankly, it was fucking sexy as hell."

"Was I on video again, or did you see it happen? Christ! Do you want a coffee or something?" I ask, walking through the hall toward the kitchen.

"Video-until I got there. Then I took over, couldn't let you have *all* the fun. A coffee is cool if you're having one too."

"I'm going to need more than one to make it through the rest of the day. I still have to do the shopping thing and get the kids from Austin's."

"Anything I can do to help? Sunday's are a free day for me." He leans against my kitchen Island.

I slip him a cup while mine is brewing. "You would just help if I asked you to, wouldn't you?"

He looks around, taking in his surroundings. "I'm of the mind if there's something I can do to help a person, and I don't what does that say about me? I'm not one to really be idle. Too many years of chasing Sofia around. I like to keep busy."

"I understand chasing a kid around. Try doing it with three. That's like right now, if I go up to their rooms and bathroom, there will be clothes and towels on the floor because I haven't even started cleaning where I've had Dante. As of last night, the girls still weren't talking to me, and Crew still had a billion questions." I sigh, rounding the counter to sit beside Jarrett.

"What sort of questions? Let's start there. I mean, it's only going to get more complicated the longer you let it fester."

"I'm not sure if I'm ready for the answers myself. This thing was so unexpected. Yet, all the kids and their parents are talking about it. I figured I had time to just let it be and have fun. Things didn't really go as planned." I'm rambling; it's something I do when I'm nervous or don't have all the answers.

"Hey, who says we can't be straightforward *and* still have fun? You and me? We're in exploration mode. Exploring our options, our bodies." Jarrett pushes my hair behind my ear before gently kissing the nape of my neck. Did I

RESOLUTION

mention I was still rocking his tee-shirt since he managed to mangle my blouse last night?

"But to answer Crew's questions would change this." I point between the two of us. "He made me promise him during the divorce that I'd let him meet any guy that may come into my life, and there could be a potential anything with them. Well, my *precious* twelve-year-old says when should he meet you if I'm having *relations* with you. He's too smart for his own good."

Jarrett shrugs. "So then, I meet him. I'm not afraid of a twelve-year-old boy. If I were him, I'd want to make sure the guy my mom was seeing was not a prick too. We do it someplace neutral, but where he feels safe but not threatened by my presence. As for your girls, they're smarter than you think and are probably chewing on this too."

"They're so mad at me for not letting them go with their dad. I did find out where he wanted to take them and would have said no if he had called like he was supposed to. Seattle, because apparently there was a baby shower this weekend. I hate telling the kids no, but if I let him take the girls, it would have been a fight to get them home. Crew won't go, or I'd feel better about it."

"So let me get this straight, he's remarried with a baby on the way, but you can't see a man without lip? Winnie, you can't do this to yourself. You have the right to companionship, to finding a partner. Someone who can help heal the hole Brad left behind."

"Honestly, I'm afraid of loving or giving myself to someone completely again. In the last four or five years, I can't even keep it straight now. We slept in separate rooms. In the last four years, we never touched one another. The girls were two, and Crew was five. Even then, Crew knew something wasn't right. If it wasn't for my friends, I would have been in a mental hospital, I'm sure. Chasing a three old around while pregnant with twins then after they were born. It was a lot. I told him after the girls were so early I didn't want to birth anymore of my own but that we could adopt, and he gave up."

"He's an idiot. You gave him three children, and he couldn't be happy with that? He should have been around, been present in your marriage. You've spent a long time being a mom, and you will always be that, but you need to remember that you are more than the sum of your parts. Mother, divorcee, friend. These are labels we take on, faces we hold, so others feel better. What really matters is how you feel. If you're unhappy, it will trickle down into your kids. Trust me. I spent more than twenty years being all about Sofia, and I still managed to miss the scumbag she married. We can't just focus on our kids, or they become the only thing we see, and then they leave, and you are left trying to find out who you are without them. Don't make my mistake, don't get so lost you can't find your way back to you."

"I'm trying. Going to lunch with you was taking a big step, and you see how many years it took me to do that."

"I'm honored you took a chance on me. Now, why not take a chance that your kids are as smart and gracious as their beautiful mom?" He kisses me, a lingering panty drenching kiss. "Now, how would you like to use me for the day?"

I stand, putting my cup down, and step away. "In a way, I don't have the time for."

"Do you want me to go?" He watches me.

"No, but I have to shower then figure out what shopping has to be done. So, tell me, what do you plan on doing?"

"I could help get things here in order while you're in the shower. Laundry started, beds made that sort of thing. This way, it's one less thing you have to do. Or I can go over your meal plans and write your grocery list."

"I hear cleaning, laundry, even writing out a grocery list. You know what I don't hear?" I ask, pulling off his shirt and dropping it to the floor as I start walking away. If he's planning to stick around, I might as well use him right.

Chapter 18- Jarrett

Seriously? It takes my brain a moment to register that she's stripping *for* me. Through her house, I move, my mouth dry, and my palms sweat. I've been playing with her, teasing her as much as I've been teased. Only now, when the real prospect of bedding this woman is unavoidable, I'm finding myself *nervous*? Somewhere between the dining room and the hallway, I manage to lose my shirt. Seeing her head up a flight of stairs, I kick off my shoes at the base before stalking up them after her. At the top, I'm faced with two halls, one ahead and one behind.

"Winnie?" I call as my eyes dart around. I spy movement out the corner of my right eye and turn my head; there's an open door. Deciding that is where my prey has gone, I take the needed steps to enter. I glance around the womanless room. Queen sized bed, picture window, 55-inch television. I'm a man-I notice things like this. Hearing water running, I zero in-cutting left. When I enter the large white and grey suite, I find that the shower has glass walls and is occupied by a divine beauty who's just begun to soap up her body.

She opens her eyes then gives me a smile and a nod. I lose my clothes; you don't have to tell me twice. Stepping into the steamy shower, I smile.

"Need a bit of help?"

"What kind of help can you give me?" She asks devilishly. Taking the loofah from her hand, I turn us, so she's facing the one tile wall, and the water isn't drowning us both. I start to slowly scrub her down, starting with her shoulders and then her back. Pushing back into me, her ass bumps my cock, and it starts to come to life. She lets out a little moan when my hands round her hips, and I start rubbing her breasts with one hand while the other teases her throbbing clit.

"We don't have any condoms," I say, kissing her shoulders.

"Birth control and menopause. Periods are sporadic. We're good; I promise you that. Unless you've got something to tell me." She turns her head to look at me.

"No, I'm good, I just- I didn't want to assume." I turn her to face me, letting the water rinse all down us. "If we're going to do this, I want to see your face."

"You can see my face. Tell me, what are you going to do now?"

Her confidence and defiance have my heart rattling against my ribs. Kissing her, I pin her to the wall, lifting her leg to the small ledge lets my wandering fingers have access. She's wet, but not nearly enough. My thumb circles her clit as my fingers tease her open. Winnie wraps her arms around my neck and shoulders going up on her tiptoe, thrusting her pelvis toward me. She's urging me to keep going. Licking her nipples, I glide my fingers into her, and she gasps, digging those pretty pink nails into me. The bit of pain makes me go at her faster, deeper; I find that little rough patch inside her and stoke. Her head falls back, and a long moan escapes her lips as her walls constrict around my long thick fingers. I can't take it anymore. Before she can come down from her orgasm, I pull my fingers from her, and lifting her legs up and over my forearms; I penetrate her.

Her body lifts as I work myself in, inch by inch. "Are you okay?" I ask as she tenses up.

"I'm fine, just don't *stop*." She kisses me and crosses her ankles behind my ass, pulling me into her further. I accustom myself to her. She's different than Gabby. In every conceivable way. Her body is more pliable, softer in all the right places. She doesn't just fuck me; rather, she's letting me work for both our needs. She yelps as I thrust, we slip down the wall, and soon I'm on my knees with her ass in my hands. She wiggles against my fingers, and I remember her making mention of ass play. Spreading her cheeks, I press my fingers against her tight little hole. Winnie starts to grind on me, and it feels so damn good.

RESOLUTION

Next thing I know, she's pressing her hand against my fingers, urging me to further explore. Between the water and the soap, I'm able to enter her here too. Her moans become ravenous as I fill both her holes. Unable to hold back anymore, I warn her I'm going to come.

"Do it." She pants, kissing me hard. I explode, pounding deep inside, my hot cum filling her up. I can't think, can't move as my whole body releases its frustrations. My back stings from her claw marks, and the bites she's made on my neck and shoulders, I'm sure, will be leaving marks. I lean back against the glass, panting, watching her.

"That's. That." She's panting, trying to catch her breath. "Can we do that every day?"

"I'm not opposed to it." I laugh. "You should see the shower in my other place. I've installed a bench along one wall, and there's enough floor space for me to lay down in it. If you can sneak away, it's only ever me now. Especially after noon time." I rub my fingers up and down her leg.

"You promise to fuck me like you just did, and I'll find the time."

"That's a deal. Guess I'm going to have to start with the master and work my way out." I chuckle.

"You make sure it's ready, and I'll bring *everything* else."

"That won't be much of a problem." I lean forward, which causes her to have to lean back.

"Seems someone hasn't had enough yet. Shower or bed and toys?"

"Toys, huh? What have you got in mind?" I've got her almost on her back.

"That depends. Do you like playing with my ass, or do you want to feel the vibration against your nuts?"

"Something says I'm about to get schooled. That's alright. I'm a fast learner and am sure to blow the curve." I stand up, pulling her to her feet.

"We'll see about that." She grabs a towel throwing one to me. "You go to the bed. I'll meet you there."

With a smile, I watch her trot off and into what I'm to assume is the closet. I finish drying off and pulling back the blankets, I get myself to the center of her bed. A few moments pass, and I start to stroke my cock, keeping it ready for her. She emerges, and in her hands are two toys. One is a long black thing with three bulbous sections. The other is similar to the wand vibrator. Only it's got what looks like a tongue on the end. I swallow as she smiles.

"You okay there?" She asks, stopping at her nightstand. She drops the toys on the bed.

Picking up the black one, I look at her. "I'm pretty sure I know what that one is, but this one has me at a loss."

"Unless you like someone playing with your ass, that's for me." She pulls lube out of her nightstand.

"Maybe some other time." I quirk a brow. "So you want us to fuck while this thing is inside you? Okay, I'm open to that."

"Trust me. You'll love it." She climbs into bed. "How you want me will depend on how we do this."

I lick my lips. "Whatever way you want to go, I'm good with. I like you on top of me, or we could go from behind or with you on your side? I'm open to pretty much anything so long as I get to bury my cock back inside you. You felt fantastic."

"You have to hold this one in or at least my ass to make sure it stays in place. So, how do you want me?"

"Let's get this in position, then I'll figure the rest out." I take the anal toy from her and the lubricant. "Come here and present that pretty little ass."

Winnie straddles my lap with her ass facing me and head down. My cock dances. It seems we agree this is a great view. "Do you need me to walk you through this, or do you got it?"

I lean forward, kissing and nibbling her butt cheek. "I got this."

I crack the top on the lube and get the toy good and slick, then take a bit more, and with my fingers, apply it to her. Spreading her open, she wiggles, and I touch the tip to her hole, pressing in slightly, then pulling back from the tension. I press again, and she grips the sheets as the first nub disappears inside, then the second. I twist the toy, pulling it back out to the first nub, then go back in. Her ass raises as I do this several times fucking her with the toy. I get it into the base, and she arches her back exquisitely.

"You okay?" I ask, running my hand around her hip and up to her breast.

"Would you quit asking if I'm okay? I'm fine. You seem to like this position."

I push her forward. As soon as my cock lines up with the rest of her, I grasp it and lead it to her center. The fit is far tighter than it was in the shower. "Fuck." I groan. "I didn't think you could feel any better."

"We're just getting started." She says, reaching for the other toy and some kind of remote.

I feel her set the toy against her clit and start it. The vibrations and the licking motion against my shaft as I slip in and out of her is crazy. I have to lift her, I want access to those ripe round tits, but with the other toy in place, I need to use my thighs to keep it there. She bounces up and down, and just when I thought I have had all I can handle the anal toy starts moving! Setting off vibrations of its own and thrusting inside her. I think my head exploded for a moment there. I get that kick in the balls but don't want to stop. Pulling out of her, I grab her leg and turn her over. Getting her knees into her chest, I pound her harder, matching the rhythm of our little helpers. She drops her legs, spreading them open wide, and the resistance finishes me. I cum as I kiss her, pressing the anal toy deeper into her as my weight hits her on the bed. She writhes under me while I fill her up, making a mess of her and the sheets. Spent I collapse, pulling her into and on top of me. Just because I'm not fucking her doesn't me I can't still fill her to the brim. She's

RESOLUTION

hot, tight, and just feels too good to part from just yet.

Chapter 19- Winnie

It's been a long week. Sunday-after, Jarrett and I had our sex marathon- he helped me clean up the house and get laundry started. Then we went to the grocery store *together*. Taking his truck instead of going to get my car. Crew called a few times, and I was honest about who I was with. Told him we'd figure it out together, which lead me to making dinner instead of going out tonight like a usual Saturday.

Jarrett and I still had lunch on Tuesday after therapy. Apparently, we're both supposed to be starting *group therapy*. That will be odd. We've still had our phone conversations all week at bedtime, but other than Tuesday, we haven't had time to meet up.

"Girls take Lulu out back. She's yapping at the door." I holler for Ivy and Iris.

RESOLUTION

"Mom, somebody just pulled into the drive. He's got flowers and gift bags!" Crew shouts.

"Okay, Crew, I'm coming," I call, checking on the pork chops. The girls come running through the house as I head for the door. "Girls, chill!" I holler before opening the door. "Welcome to the zoo."

"Is it okay to feed the monkeys?" He smiles, presenting a dozen long stem pink and white roses to me.

"Thank you, and if they keep running in my house, they are going to bed without dinner. Please come in." I move so Jarrett can come in, and Crew is standing there leaning against the wall.

"Jarrett Brooks, I'm Crew McCormick, the man of this house."

Jarrett doesn't miss a beat as he steps to and towers over my son. He extends his right hand. "It's a pleasure to meet you, Crew. Your mother speaks well of you." He holds up the small blue gift bag. "I was raised you never come empty-handed to a person's home. Especially if they're gracious enough to feed you."

"She's feeding you. I'm not allowed to help since I caught the kitchen on fire when I was seven."

"Speaking of feeding, dinner is not quite done, and I need to get these in a vase. Crew, would you go grab your sisters?" I nod my head to Jarrett. "You can follow me

I'm in the kitchen, finishing up dinner when Jarrett finally comes in. "You okay?"

"I'm good." He watches me. I know *that* look. I've seen it enough over the course of the week.

"Don't even think about it. You'll make me burn the food."

"I *so* wanted to kiss you hello but felt it would have been inappropriate."

"He knows we kiss. He asked. I figured best to tell the truth."

He moves past the counter and straight to me. Pulling me from the stove, he wraps me into his arms and kisses me. My hands go into his hair and rake his scalp as he bends me back ever so slightly. Letting me catch my breath, he laughs shortly. "Hello." He smiles as I right myself.

"Hello to you too."

"Really? Around the food? Can't you do that somewhere else?" Crew cringes, and I smile. He's still holding the gift bag.

"Have you looked inside the bag yet?" Jarrett asks just as Iris and Ivy come into the room.

"I was waiting for them." Crew points over his shoulder. The girls stop beside Crew, and before I can make introductions, he does. He points at Ivy first. She's in a purple shirt with a gold heart. "This is Ivy; she talks a lot." Then to Iris, who is in gray with a gold star and book in her hand. "And Iris, she's the quieter of the two and always has a book close by."

Ivy speaks up. "So, you like our mom, huh? We have a dad, you know, and we're *not* looking for a replacement."

RESOLUTION

"Ivy Kathleen! Jarrett, I'm sorry, I'm not sure what has come over her." I say, trying not to burn dinner.

"It's alright." Jarrett smiles. "There's nothing wrong with being honest." Walking toward the girls, he holds out two purple bags, one long the other wide. "I do like your mom, and I'm not looking to replace anybody. Though I was hoping we could possibly be friends." Ivy is handed the wide bag and Iris the long.

"You got us gifts?" Ivy asks curiously, looking over at me.

"Of course. As I told your brother, I was raised to never be empty-handed the first time I come to a person's home for an occasion like dinner. Your mom got those roses over there, and these things are for each of you. They aren't extravagant, just my way of saying thank you for having me in your home."

"Daddy isn't going to like this," Ivy says, and Iris shoves her.

"Shut up and accept the gift." Iris and Crew look at one another before opening their bags.

"Mom, he got me a reed case with extra reeds for my sax." Crew says excitedly.

"Drum sticks that change colors. This is awesome. Thank you." Iris looks at Jarrett with a smile.

"Yeah, thank you."

Ivy is watching like she doesn't know who these two are. "Ivy, you're being rude. Open your gift and say thank you."

Iris being over her sister's drama takes the bag from Ivy and opens it. "This is fitting." She says, and Crew starts laughing, turning it for me to see. It's a shirt that says *Nothing But Treble*.

"Ivy, what do you say?"

"Thank you, Mister Brooks," Ivy says with gritted teeth. He couldn't expect to get all three of them on his side that easy.

"You are quite welcome, say if you'd rather not wear it, I'm sure I can fashion a frame, and you could put it on the wall. In the basement."

"Thank you, but no thank you," Ivy says, and I'm sure I'm going to kill her.

"Suit yourself." Jarrett turns his attention back to me. "Something sure does smell good. Anything I can do to help?"

"Everything is just about done. Kids, go wash up, please." Crew and Iris push Ivy from the room, and I look over at Jarrett. "I'm so sorry. They do have better manners than that."

"This isn't about manners. It's about territory. You are their mother. Like she said, they have a father, who, regardless of anything, is hanging around. Little girls cling to their daddy's and the idea of them until they're gone from this world. Like I told her, I'm not trying to replace Brad. I just wanna get to know you."

"I haven't run you off. Brad didn't, neither did the kids. So, tell me, what's the deal-breaker here? So I know the stopping point." I try to ask with a serious face but can't.

He looks at me reflectively. "I'm not sure, does the idea of dating a man about to be a grandfather toss you off at all?"

Turning off the stove, I turn toward him, wrapping my arms around his waist. "No, it's a baby I can adore but didn't have to birth. So, I can help spoil it and send it home."

He sputters a laugh. "You plan on being around four months from now?" He hugs me to him. "I like hearing that."

"I'll stay around for the baby's sake. You only know how to take care of little girls. I can't imagine you if it would be a boy. Whole different ball game."

"It is, in fact, a boy. Scott Windom Brooks-Guteriez. Though I hope she takes full custody and eliminates that s.o.b. A man that will hit his pregnant wife has no business alone with a fussy child." I can feel the underlying rage thoughts of his son-in-law produce.

"As long as she had proof, which I know she did, I saw it, but it won't be easy. Have you found the lawyer yet?" I ask as I start putting everything on serving platters.

"Yes. She's been in constant contact with Sofia, has gotten the PTO in place, and I took pictures of her bruises, which were given over. Fillipe seems to think that since he's a hotshot criminal attorney that he's untouchable. What he's failed to realize is that she's filed for divorce here in California, their state of marriage origin. Where they have been sharing dual residency for two years. He's *screwed*."

"Good, you let me know if you need help. Is she working or trying to?" I ask as Jarrett puts the platters on the table.

"She's trying to figure that out. She worked as a pattern drafter and draper for a designer in Boston the last six months. Before that, it was doing alterations in a dry cleaners. She says she doesn't know what to do. Here she is with a degree she doesn't know what to do with. You should see the way she can sew. Just beautiful stuff. She actually made her wedding gown."

"Is that what she wants to do, or does she want to do something else?"

He shrugs. "Right now, I just want her to have a healthy baby. I have space if she needs to stay with me. I can always convert the upstairs spare to a nursery. She says she doesn't want to go to the house they were gonna rent. I've got all her stuff in a storage unit across town."

"She could come work at the Salon if she wants. Help sell products or work behind the juice counter. If she doesn't stay active, she's going to have hard labor." I grab the dinnerware from the cabinets.

"She's active. Works out daily, has been fussing in the craft room, and there's Oliver Brexit. The young surfing instructor who delivers the groceries in his spare time." Jarrett's eyes roll hard.

"I take it you don't approve?"

"She's still married, and anything that could give that p.o.s. any leverage, I think, is a bad idea. She's grown, though, so she's going to do as she pleases. At least she tells me where and with who." He sighs. "At least he can't get her pregnant." Looking at the stove. "We look good to eat."

"If the kids ever get down here. Give me a second." I go to the stairs and yell up. "If you're eating, I suggest you move your ass!"

RESOLUTION

"Ivy's pouting." Crew hollers down.
"Fine, you and Iris come on down, and I'll go up."

Chapter 20- Jarrett

Ten minutes. Ten minutes of silent observation. I'm sitting at the dining room table while Iris and Crew sorta stare at me. Unable to take it anymore, I cross my eyes and stick out my tongue.

"You're *weird*," Iris says, and Crew elbows her.

"Not nice. Do you have kids?"

I chuckle at Iris's observation as I nod. "I do, a daughter, Sofia, but she's quite a bit older than you are."

"Do you want more? Because you should know mom doesn't." Iris speaks this time. "Ivy and I were hard on her."

"Well, that's a good question. Way I see it is if we." I point between us. "Got to be friends. It would be sorta like having more kids. You are at the fun stage. Babies can't talk to you, and you gotta carry them everywhere. Not you guys, you have your own budding personalities that would be great to see develop."

"Ivy will come around; it just takes her time," Iris says as Winnie and Ivy come into the room.

Winnie pushes Ivy to me. "I'm sorry for making you wait." Looking at her, it's apparent she's been crying. I feel bad for the little girl because I know she just misses her daddy.

"No problem, it gave me a moment to chat with these two."

"Let's eat," Winnie says, going to the fridge. "You two couldn't get drinks?"

"You just said to come down here, mom." Crew answers.

"It's my fault, Winnie. I can be a distraction." I say, standing. "Let me help you there as penance."

She rolls her eyes at me but pulls milk out. "What would you like? Water, soda, wine, beer, or milk?"

"I'll have what you're having." I look around. The slate grey kitchen is big and open, but the cabinets are far from the sink, where I would keep dishes and cups. "Glasses?"

"Right side of the stove. I'm having wine."

"Tall or short for them?" I ask, heading over.

"Tall for Crew short for the girls. They don't drink milk, whereas Crew could live on it." She says, grabbing juice out.

"I used to drink it by the gallon, till my first kidney stone." I grab the glasses, setting them on the counter. "They say the pain of one is comparable to childbirth. I had three."

"Christ. Grab the wine from the fridge?"

"Sure." I stop halfway there, the walls between the dining room and the kitchen blocking us. "It's going better than I expected." My hands slip around her front, and I reach into her blouse, tweaking a nipple. "You've got good kids."

"They have their moments," Winnie says, leaning back into me with a low moan.

"What time do they go to bed?" My other hand travels up her skirt, and I gently press my fingers against her panties. I can't help myself. This woman oozes confidence, and the way she performs for me at night has me on high alert.

"They have to be in bed by eleven at the latest. Crew still has to call and tell his girlfriend goodnight. They'll probably go to the basement after dinner." Her ass rubs against me.

"Hmm, I spied a very comfortable fire pit situation outside. Perhaps you can show it to me over a bottle of wine?" My middle finger ducks under her panty line, and I trace her clit. She's already getting wet. Pressing into her, I collect her juice on my finger as I swirl it inside her. Releasing her, I suck my finger, getting the tangy taste of her. "*Delicious.*"

"You're terrible." She turns to me, pulling me down to her and kissing me.

"You like it." I grab the tray with the drinks on it. "You get the door?"

***

RESOLUTION

Just as predicted, the kids went downstairs to the media room after dinner, leaving Winnie and me alone. I'm outside getting the firepit going while Winnie grabs another bottle of peach Moscato. It's barely a wine, but it does taste good. The temperature is a crisp sixty or so degrees, making it perfect fire weather. I've just sat down in the large cushy bench seat when she appears. Bottle and glasses in hand, she's in the doorway, watching me. She's barefoot now, and of course, her toes match the baby blue manicure.

"There you are." I smile, patting the seat beside me.

"Had to break up a fight about whose turn it was to pick the movie, then I guess I'm taking Crew and his girlfriend to see a movie tomorrow." She says, walking my way.

"Is it more than three hours?" I smirk as she sets the glasses and bottle down so she can snuggle into me.

"I have no idea. He picks the movie- asks her parents- then tells me. So I can take him to the store to pick up flowers and chocolates, then pick her up. I drop them off and do my shopping while they watch their movie. The girls usually watch a different movie. Then I make sure I'm back in time. *Parenthood*."

"You're telling me you don't buy a ticket and hide in the back row to keep an eye?" I put my arm around her as she grabs the throw behind us, getting it over our front. "I think I stalked all of Sofia's movie dates until she left for college. Hell, I was the chauffeur for all of her school dances. It was more cost-efficient to rent a fancy car than to pay for limo service."

"No, I haven't done that since I passed out on his first one. He looks like his dad but has more heart than Brad ever could. Crew takes his girlfriend chocolate to school when he says she's in a *mood*. He doesn't complain. Honestly, I think he is going to be the easy one. It's Ivy that worries me."

"She's young, and she misses her dad. Unfortunately, there's little you can do about that. You need to just try and keep her talking. When the talking stops, then you have a problem. I don't mean these little outbursts where she punishes you with the silent treatment. I mean when she stops coming to you. Ivy needs to know that wherever you are, you are still where she needs you."

"I don't plan to go anywhere, but life happens," Winnie says.

"Mom, can Cassie stay the night?" Crew comes outside.

"Do I look like I have stupid written across my forehead? No, your girlfriend can not stay the night." She looks from him to me. "Maybe I do have something to worry about."

"Have you had *that* talk yet?" I pull the blanket over her better, as I'd begun to unbutton her top before Crew made his appearance.

"Yeah, we had the talk and made a deal. When he's ready to go there, he comes to me, and we talk about it again, first. I had to quit smoking."

RESOLUTION

"So that's your reason? Sofia made me promise to be alive for Scotty's college years. She doesn't want him to grow up without anybody as she did."

"Keeping my almost thirteen-year-old from doing something he isn't ready for by quitting? Best decision I've made aside from divorcing Brad." Winnie laughs.

"I can't argue any of that, seeing as they both led to this moment. You in *my* arms." I kiss her gently. "Where have you been all my life?"

"Spain and Vegas before landing close by for college."

"I grew up in Sacramento, went to U.C.L.A. and Berkley, respectively. But I've been in Cherry Tree Heights for almost fifteen years. We frequent the same places, but it took a shrink's office for us to meet. It's unreal."

"Maybe so, but you've got to remember other than Saturday and Sunday, I'm usually tied down with kids from three to twelve."

"I know, but Sofia worked for Brenton Sweet for *two years*. She knows all of you by name. I used to pick her up after her shifts. It just amazes me we never once crossed paths."

"We were always so loud most people stayed away. Sofia has seen more then I'm sure she ever wanted. Always got tipped well, though. I can only imagine what she said about us." Winnie covers her face.

"That you all have no filters, talk incessantly about the sex you're *not* getting, and that *Bryce* was the sexiest man alive." I pull her into my lap.

"He's also the youngest aside from Tatum."

"Should I worry? Or have you gotten him out of your system?" I kiss her between the breasts.

"He was never really *in* my system. He used my drunken state and my really bad days and all, but like twice was in the back of a jeep. We're good as long as you keep that up."

"What? *This*?" I expose her nipple. Today's ring is vampire's teeth. I carefully glide my tongue between the teeth and flick her flesh. "Or *this*?" I rise up, my hard cock tapping her as if knocking to say hello.

"Both." She says, going for my pants. "We're going to have to be stealthy. Think you can handle that?"

My mind races back to the night she'd been drinking when she asked me about my fantasy. "Let me tell you a little story..." I smile, pulling her panties down her hips.

Chapter 21-Winnie

I should have been at therapy and my lunch date, but *instead*, I'm home with a kid. Take him to the doctor, and he's got freaking Mono! Crew's response to this... *I swear it was only a couple of times.* Apparently, Cassie has been on antibiotics for the last couple of weeks for this same thing. All I can think is, *why in the fuck is she kissing my fucking child?* Oh, let's see to infect him as well! I'm so pissed I could bite nails in two.

I'm headed for the kitchen when there's a knock on the door. Shit. Turning around, I head for the sound.

"Mom. Drink." Crew whines pitifully, like the man that he thinks he is.

"Yes, I know, Crew," I say, opening the door to see Jarrett. "Hey, sorry I wasn't able to make it."

"*Mom*."

"Okay, Crew," I say, flustered.

Jarrett looks me up and down. "You gonna just stand there, or are you gonna let me in?" He holds up a couple of plastic bags from Sweet'ums and coffee from Sweet Caroline's. I should probably mention to him that Piper owns that place.

I hold out my hand for him to go ahead, and Crew whines again. "So help me God, Crew! If you weren't kissing a girl, you wouldn't be in this situation. Shut up!"

Jarrett's shoulders rise and fall in laughter. "Where do you want me the put the food? I've got chicken soup for the kissing fool, bacon cheddar burgers, fries, and onion rings for us. Plus a slice of strawberry cheesecake for dessert."

"Kitchen, please," I say, following behind him. "He's got Mono. Then he had the nerve to tell me he didn't know how he got it until the doctor explained, then it was just a couple times. All it took was once!"

"That's how I got Sofia." He puts the coffees down, then the bags.

"*So*, not helping. We're just getting home. I've chewed through a pack of gum, and now I'm out and only got two lollis left."

"Guess it's good I'm here then." He waggles his brows at me. "You need to eat. If I need to go get you stuff, I'll go after we eat."

"I don't know what I need. All I know is we're home for at least the rest of the week or until the fever is gone. If that whining he's doing keeps up, I'm gonna be insane by tomorrow." I rub my head, trying to get the headache that's been forming to go away.

"Don't worry, I've been through this, four times actually. Sofia was a kissing fool. Hence my stalking her dates. You need to push fluids. Gatorade is always a good idea unless he likes Pedialyte. That is even better. Throat lozenges, healthy soups, nothing with creams though it causes phlegm, and the coughing will irritate him more. Popsicles." He rotates his hand. "The essentials."

"If he wasn't kissing in the first place, we wouldn't have this issue," I say, walking around the counter to grab a tray.

"If you don't want me to kiss, maybe you shouldn't be having sex out back." Crew says, walking into the kitchen.

"Little boy, you are working my nerves. You have no idea what you are talking about."

"It wasn't cold enough to need a blanket, and you were facing him. Even the girls saw."

"Crew, living room. Go. Now!"

"Can I at least have my drink?"

"Yes, take the damn drink and go!" I'm on the verge of tears.

Crew walks to the fridge pulling out a Gatorade, then leaves the room, and I let my head hit the counter.

I feel Jarrett's hands run up my back and into my shoulders. He gives me a firm squeeze, attempting to rub out the tension. "Well, that's one less conversation we have to have."

"Seriously! Nope, I am not talking about this. I'm taking the infected kid his soup, then I'm gonna come back in here and cry until I feel better." I grab the tray setting it on the counter, then go for a bowl because he won't eat all the soup at once.

I take Crew everything he needs and tell him after he eats to try and sleep. By the time I make it back to the kitchen, Jarrett has the other food set out on the counter, and he's poured me a tall glass of wine.

"I'm sorry for snapping," I say, sitting beside him.

Pushing the wine toward me, he smiles. "It's *okay*. I can only imagine how bad I was back when Sofia first caught it. She was ten. I was ready to pour a foundation and murder the twelve-year-old boy she had been kissing on the playground."

"That's bad," I say, taking a drink. "I have to take him back next week so they can check his tonsils. Doc said they may have to go."

"Oh, that is great for the first two or three days. They can hardly talk from the swollen tongue, and when they do, it's hilarious. So as not to be made fun of for sounding ridiculous, they stay nice and quiet. It was the most peace I'd had since she was still taking naps."

"That is so mean. I'm just trying to figure out the schedule with all the other kids. Thankfully, Brent can handle them today, but I doubt he can do it for the next few weeks *and* work."

"Well, can I be of some help?" He chomps on an onion ring. "My afternoons are flexible."

"I don't know, I don't know how that would even work."

"I mean, what exactly do you need done? Dropping off kids at activities? I can do that. I'm a very safe driver when I'm not watching you. If that doesn't fly with your friends, I can come here, sit with him. I can give you a break, so you can take a bath, regroup. Doing this alone will wear you down, and if you get sick, then what?"

"Oh, the whole thing explodes— no, it's not my friends I'm worried about. It's the kids, and well, *you*, to be honest. Addyson and Allyson have ballet during the week. They're the three-year-olds. Iris and Ivy have volleyball Monday, Wednesday, and Friday with dance and cheer Tuesdays and Thursdays. Rumor is with the girls at volleyball, and Echo has gymnastics when the other three are at volleyball, and she goes to dance and cheer with mine. Rumor just sits with me and does her homework when she doesn't have anything."

"Okay, so you write it up. It's been a few years since I've had to run like that, but I'm sure I'm up for the challenge."

I grab him by the shoulders and try to shake him. "Do you have to be so damned perfect?"

"I'm hardly perfect. A perfect man would not be trying to figure out how to fuck you on this counter with your kid in the other room."

"No, that's *exactly* what the perfect man would be trying to do when he knows momma is flipping her shit and needs a release in the worst kind of way."

"You eat your food, and I'll eat *you*. Just sit down right here behind the counter." He grabs my ass and then inches my yoga pants down to my hips.

"Jarrett, you're killing me. There isn't any way I'm eating while you're doing *that*."

"Watch me."

"Oh, I plan to do just that."

Chapter 22-Jarrett

"It's an awful lot of trouble," Sofia says as I'm grabbing my wallet off the counter. I look at her questioningly. "What you're going through for Winne. I mean, haven't you just started dating her?"

I look at her. "Have you got to have an opinion on everything? Little girl, I've kept my opinions to myself about your recent actions, have I not?" I smooth back my hair putting on my baseball cap. "Can't you do me the same courtesy?"

"Different animals. I'm just having a bit of fun before the baby comes, and Oliver has been really great for that. It's been like old times."

"Old times? What crazy are you going on about?"

"Boy daddy, you never did keep good track of the boys I dated. I saw Oliver through most of

Junior year. Then he moved away. I spent four months crying about it."

"I remember the crying. I remember a lot of chocolate and ice cream disappearing faster than I could stock it."

"Yeah, if he hadn't moved *this*." She grabs her ever-growing belly. "Would have been his."

"You're not divorced *yet*. It could look bad."

"Not as bad as his running around and beating my ass. I think I'm good." She hugs me. "Daddy, I just hope that you've thought this through and that if you are serious about her, you leave *mom* the fuck alone."

I look down at her in surprise.

"Oh yeah, I know you and mom have been screwing for the last few years on and off. I didn't say anything because it wasn't hurting anybody. Now though, you got insta-family going on. Just be sure you know what you're doing."

I kiss her head. "You trying to parent me, are ya?"

"Somebody's got to do it."

"I'm going. If you need anything—"

"I'll call Oliver." She winks at me and shoves me out the door.

That conversation cut right into my coffee stop, meaning by the time I get to Winnie's, she's already got the girls in the Traverse and is about to pull out of the driveway. I pull up alongside her, and it's a pass by while she hands me the keys.

"He's still in bed. I'll call after lunch." She blows me a kiss and is zipping down the road.

RESOLUTION

This has been a semblance of the last two weeks. Since we can both dictate our schedules, we've been trading off. I hold down the fort on the days she goes to work. It took an act of congress to talk her into going back, but I could see her losing her mind being home. She conceded, and toady is her second day leaving me with Crew all day. She doesn't want to leave Crew alone, so every morning, I come out and just sorta keep watch. When he wakes up, I set out pills and make him a protein shake since it's about the only food he's swallowing these days. Doctor Grissom, the ear, nose, and throat specialist, says the tonsils need to come out, so Winnie is stressing over that.

In the house, I have come to finally meet Lulu, the family pug. Every morning is a surprise as she meets me in a new ridiculous outfit. Today is no different. Today she is dressed in a plaid sweater with pearls. Yesterday it was a taco for Tuesday. Them little girls have an imagination, that's for sure. I set up the coffee pot and hear Crew moving upstairs, just as I'm pouring the first cup of sludge. I'm horrible with drip pots. I have a Keurig at home to avoid this crazy.

I hear the TV in the living room startup. Curious as to why he hasn't come into the kitchen, I wander out. He's sitting there flipping channels, Lulu in his lap.

"How you feeling?"

He grunts at me.

"That good, huh? You want your shake and pill?"

I get a nod. As I go to make the shake, I feel the ground beneath my feet vibrate. Suddenly the whole house shifts, and I make a dash for Crew, pulling him into me and us into the doorway. The quake doesn't last long, but it manages to drop the ceiling fan just a few feet from where Crew had been sitting. He clings to me as Lulu whines.

"You okay?" I ask, feeling his heart racing as quickly as my own. We don't usually get quakes in this area. I honestly can't remember the last one that I really *felt*, let alone that shook the house.

He shakes his head against me. "I'm scared." He manages to get out, but it wasn't easy for him.

My thoughts are all over the place. I need to call his mom. I need to call Sofia. I pull up my messenger and put them in a group call. I know that the phones may be out, but hopefully, this will go through. It rings. "I'm getting your mom on the horn."

Winnie picks up. "Hey, is are you all okay?" She sounds frantic. I drop the phone down so she can see her son, as my adrenaline pumps faster. Sofia hasn't answered yet. "Shit, um, let me get Chance to take over, and I'll come home. We've got to close up anyway. Are you okay?"

"Winnie, Sofia isn't answering. I-I need to go to the house. I'm packing Crew up. Meet us there?"

"Yeah, go. Just *be* careful."

"Yeah, I lo- I'll see you soon." I hang up the phone. I get Crew pulled together, as in I get shoes on him and grab the dog. I keep trying my daughter, my fear building with every second that passes by. Is she hurt? Is the baby okay? Christ, did I almost tell Winnie *I love you*?

Pulling up to the house, I see that the porch stairs are split. "Crew, stay put." I bark, not meaning to, as I jump out of the barley in park truck. I clear the stairs and the crack heading into the house. "Sofia!" I scream her name. "Baby? Where are you?" Looking around, I can see things are knocked off the mantle. The house groans as I look around- the den is empty, dining room, kitchen. I call for her again, trying to reconcile the damage. That's when I see the movement in the back of the house. That kitten starts crying. Following the sound, my heart stops as I see Sofia on the floor. Down I go flipping the coffee table in my way. I pull her into me, and she moans. I scoop her and the kitten up, feeling another vibration. I have two choices, risk going back through the house or out the picture windows. Grabbing the throw on the couch, I cover them and myself as best I can, and running to the windows, I smash them. My arm and shoulder stings, but I get us out as the next wave hits. I keep running toward the back of the yard as the creaking continues. At the edge of the property, I drop and watch as the lower level succumbs. The house begins to collapse—Sofia murmurs as I cling to her, trying to catch my ragged breath.

"I got you, baby, I got you."

Chapter 23- Winnie

Getting to Jarrett's was not easy in any way, shape, or form. Electric poles are down. Chance is doing damage control at the salon. Our front windows came down with the first quake. I called the girl's teacher on my way to Crew and Jarrett. Everyone is okay. The school has them doing evacuations one room at a time. I make it to Jarrett's just in time to see the house crumble to the ground.

"Crew!" I scream, getting out of the car after barely throwing it into park.

A door opens on Jarrett's truck, and I see Crew with Lulu. I rush to and pull him into me. I'm sure I'm squeezing him too hard, but I don't really care at the moment.

"He went into the house." Crew barely manages to get out.

RESOLUTION

Christ. "Crew, I need you to sit right here. I need to go make sure they made it out the back."

He nods at me, and I shut the door. Walking toward the side of the house, I'm trying to be careful and not get smashed like a bug. I finally make it around the house and see Jarrett on the ground with Sofia in his arms. There's blood everywhere.

He's rocking her when he sees me. "I can't wake her up. I'm afraid to move her."

I run to him and drop to the ground. Looking her over. She's got blood coming from her head. "We've got to get her to the hospital. We can take my car that way, you can sit in the back with her, and we have room for Crew. The streets are a mess waiting on the EMT isn't an option."

He nods, lifting her barely. That's when I see the gashes on his arm. He looks like he's gonna lose her but sucks it up; and stands. "We're right behind you."

"Is this her kitten?" I ask him. It's wrapping itself around me.

"That's Midnight. She's been taking care of it."

Up the cat goes into my arms. "Let's go." I take off for the car with Jarrett right behind me. I open the door for him before going to get Crew. "Come on, buddy. I need you to walk for me." I grab Lulu. Once we're at the car, I hand her and Midnight to Crew before shutting the door. Checking Jarrett and Sofia before shutting the door, I'm around the car and headed for the hospital.

It takes us longer than I wanted it to, but with power lines down and roads with cracks in them, it's just a mess. Homes are crashing to the ground. It's devastation. Out of the car, I'm opening the door. Then running inside to get somebody.

"I've got a pregnant woman with a bleeding head!" I shout, running into the emergency room. More than one nurse follows me out with a gurney. We run to the car where Jarrett is sitting with her in his arms. They take Sofia one way and Jarrett the other. I'm left standing outside alone, trying to figure out what to do.

My phone starts going off beside Crew, and he hands it to me. It's a group call with everyone.

"Hello?" I answer and hear all five talk at once.

"Where are you?" Piper's frantic.

"Is Crew okay?" There's Tatum.

"I'll get the girls-they're canceling classes." Brenton swoops in.

"They can come to my house, fuck. Are you okay?" Bryce is looking like he's trying to see past me.

"Win- I'm waiting on EMS. I'm stuck in my truck, wound up in a ditch." Austin groans. He's got blood on his head and face.

"Jesus, Austin!" Tatum says.

"Crew and I are okay," I say, spotting the blood in my backseat. "Um-we're-ah."

"Winnie? Are you okay? What's wrong?" Piper asks. I hear her but trying to answer her is not as easy as it should be.

"Win?" Tatum calls.

RESOLUTION

"Winnie? What?" Bryce asks, and I can hear their voices as they overlap. It isn't until I feel arms wrap around me that I snap back, seeing Crew has hugged me tightly.

I wrap an arm around him and glance back at the video on my phone. "Sorry, we're at the hospital. Jarrett had Crew, so I could work. Sofia's head is bleeding really bad. Jarrett is cut up, and his house is split in half with part of it on the ground."

"But you and Crew are okay?" Tatum asks again.

"Yes, we're fine. I just need someone to get the girls."

"Isaiah is there. Can you find him? I'm trying to get Jeremiah, Clara, and Dante. School is giving me grief." Piper says.

"I'll find him." Everyone is talking over the other. "I'm going inside. Austin, let me know when you're here and if everyone else is okay when you see them." I say, hanging up. "Grab Lulu, and I'll take Midnight. We've got to find Isaiah, Jarrett, and Sofia. You okay?"

He shrugs his shoulders, and inside, we go looking for people.

"We're here for Isaiah O'Reilly," I say, stopping at the desk.

"Are you a relative?" The little orderly asks.

"I'm his aunt."

"Birthday?"

"November twelfth of two-thousand and two."

"Name?"

"Winnie McCormick." Knowing good and well, my name is on his next of kin list.

The woman hands me two badges. One for me and one Crew. "He's in room fifteen."

With a nod, Crew and I are headed for a set of double doors that pop open as we get to them. I find room fifteen, and the curtain is open.

"Isaiah, are you okay?" I ask, walking over to the bed.

"A light fell on me. The doctor said they have to wait for the x-rays to come back. They think my wrist is broken."

"Christ. Your mom is trying to get the others from school. Was there a lot of damage?"

"Enough, but I was one of the lucky ones." He chuckles.

"Lucky one? Isaiah James O'Reilly, you could have been killed." I squeal. "I'm going to get you out of here and show you lucky."

Before I can say another word, I'm being tapped on the shoulder. Turning, I see a nurse with blood down the side of her scrubs. "Excuse me, is your name Winnie?"

"Yes?"

"The man in ten is adamant he knows you." She points a few curtains down.

Christ. "Um, okay. Crew stay with Isaiah. Just sit and don't move." I say, following the nurse to room ten. Walking into the room, I see Jarrett fighting with the nurses about staying in bed. "Would you quit acting like a child and sit down to let them take care of you?"

"Winnie!" He slurs my name as he pulls on the lines in his arm. "Tell them I'm fine... I need to

RESOLUTION

get to Sofia, my baby is having a baby. Will you have my baby?" He almost falls as they push him down and pull up the rails.

"Ma'am, are you his wife?" The nurse or doctor, I'm not even sure at this point, asks, looking at me and the kitten. "You can't have animals here. This is a hospital, *not* a vet's office."

"Listen here, I'm with this man, his daughter, who of which I have no idea where they've taken, my nephew is down the hall, and my brother is on his way. I wasn't about to leave a cat and dog in my car, so I could be charged with endangerment or whatever the fuck you would try. Second, if I put them down, they will be fighting, so shut the fuck up and do you God damned job."

"Th-that's my girl," Jarrett says as his head lobs to one side. For fuck's sake, what did they give him?

"Now, can someone please tell me what is wrong with him?"

"He presented with multiple lacerations to his right bicep and forearm. We are trying to remove the debris, which we believe to be glass, from the wounds while staying the massive amount of blood he's lost. We've administered IV fluids and plasma to try and restore the balance. As well as a morphine drip for pain and to relax him." The doctor shows himself.

"I'm itchy." Jarrett chuckles, looking at me then at his arm. "I can't-" He tries to lift the arm. "It's all floppy." He looks back at me. "Can you love a floppy armed man?"

I walk closer to him. "I need you to do something for me. I need you to let the doctor and nurses get all the glass out of you so we can go see Sofia. Isaiah is right down the hall waiting on x-ray's to come back, and Austin is on his way. He's also bleeding from the head. The girls are okay. Brent is picking them up from school. So, for now, I need you to listen and help out. Let them finish with you and get you back up to where you should be, then they'll let you out of this bed. Can you do that?" I speak as if he is a toddler.

"Can I have a kiss first?" He makes a fish face and kissy noises.

Lord, help me! I hold Jarrett's face in my hands and kiss him good and hard. It's sloppy, but if it will make him listen, I don't fucking care.

Chapter 24- Jarrett

My eyes open to bright white lights, beeping machines, and burning pain in my right arm. I squint to adjust my sight and realize I'm in the hospital. They've taken my shirt, and I'm propped up in a sling. My mouth tastes like a cat shit in it.

"Ugh-" I stick out my tongue and hear whining. Looking down the length of me, I see the pearls wearing Lulu and Crew, just staring at me. He's still in his pj's and looks like I feel. "Where's your mom?" My head feels like it's splitting open behind my eyes.

"Everywhere. Isaiah is getting a cast. Austin is here. She's fighting with the nurses about your daughter too."

I pull forward and feel the tug of the lines in my arm. "Damnit. Crew, can you hand me the call button? Please?"

Crew grabs the call button. "Do you love her? You asked her to have your baby."

I stare at him for a moment, and my slurred confessions bubble to the surface. Crew is watching me, and I'm not sure what to say. "I-" I stop, and he raises a brow putting the call light in my hand. "I care about her, and today I realized that it's not a crush situation. I would like to talk to her-the medicine they gave me-it may have had me saying things that I've thought about but weren't ready to say." I answer as honestly as I can. "I know that making sure she and you guys were okay is my priority."

"UGH! She came in at the same fucking time as her father. She's pregnant. Has a head wound. You can't be so fucking dense that you can't find her!" Winnie's squealing at someone.

Looking at Crew, he holds out his hand as if presenting her. "*This* has been going on for *hours*."

I almost laugh at the way he hisses out the complaint. I hit the call button, and the light outside my room goes bright. "Winnie!" I holler over the cacophony of noises around me.

Winnie opens the curtain but doesn't come any closer. She's just watching me with a guilt-stricken look. "You're awake. How do you feel? Crew, you were supposed to come to get me."

"Don't blame him. He was filling me in," I say with a sheepish smile. "I'm okay. You don't have to keep watch. I'll get to Sofia just as soon as I talk to the idiot doctor that sedated me."

"They had to, you lost too much blood, and we couldn't keep you in the bed." Winnie looks

RESOLUTION

from me to Crew. "Go check on Isaiah and Austin, will ya?"

"*Mom!*" Crew whines.

"*Please.*"

"*Fine.*" Crew says, walking from the room, and Winnie comes further in.

"I tried, and I've been trying. They won't give me anything. I'm so sorry."

"It's the law, and you're asking for Brooks, not Brooks-Guteriez, her married name. It's okay, I'll get it sorted. I'm just glad you are okay-I-" I'm cut off as the curtain draws back, and I'm looking at Gabby.

"Jerrett? Oh, my God!" She's at my bedside and trying to touch. I attempt to pull away as she goes on. "I saw the house and rushed over. I'm still down as your and Sofie's emergency contacts. She's asking after you. Oh, I'm so happy you're okay."

"Sofia? You've seen her?" I ask, only hearing that my baby wants me.

"Of course, she's in labor and delivery, upstairs. They had to stitch her up, give her some medication to stop her contractions, but they're okay- we just need-" She stops, finally seeing Winnie. "I'm sorry, who are you?"

"Gabby, shut up, and let a person get a word in edgewise." I snap. "Winnie McCormick, this is my ex-wife Gabrellia Santina."

Winnie sticks her hand out to Gabby. "It's nice to meet you."

"I'm sorry, but are you fucking my husband?" Gabby says, and I jump in.

"Ex-husband, since nineteen ninety-five." I look at Winnie, begging her to understand.

"Yeah, okay, so why was I riding your cock four weeks ago?"

I stutter. I can't form the words- can't defend my actions. Winnie nods her head, pulling her hand back.

"I'm glad Sofia is okay. I was worried about her." Winnie smiles at Gabby then looks at me. "I need to go check on everyone else that is here. You can let me know when you get out and what room." She kisses me. "I'll see you soon."

"I'm sorry," I whisper to her.

"Brent is making room at the house for you and Sofia for when she's allowed to come home." With one more quick kiss, Winnie is out the curtain and leaving.

Gabby turns on me, fury in her eyes. "You what- when were you gonna tell me? Next month after I rode you like a bull?"

"Gabby, I'm- no, you know what, I don't need to explain myself here. Go back to Chester and stop coming around me. What we do- it's not healthy. It's not fair to you or to me. It's certainly not fair to your fiancé."

"You don't know what you're-" She stops as the nurse finally comes in.

"I don't want this woman here. Can you please see that she's removed from my lists?" I say, and Gabby clutches her purse to her body.

"Ma'am, if you'll please." The nurse points her out. With a huff, she vacates the room.

"Thank you. Now, as for *my* daughter."

RESOLUTION

***

It's about four when they finally get an orderly to transfer me upstairs to see Sofia. Disconnected from all the tubes and wires, I'm left with sixty-seven stitches from my wrist to my shoulder. Seems plate glass windows and human flesh aren't compatible. Who knew? In a sling and still rather stoned, the hospital, not wanting to let me walk, transported me in a wheelchair. I'm pushed into Sofia's room and see her lying on the bed, a blanket over her lap, and her belly on full display. I can hear the monitors and the unmistakable sound of my grandson's heartbeat.

"Baby?" I say as I'm wheeled right up to her. I grasp her hand.

"Da-daddy?" She whispers, opening her eyes. "What happened to you?"

"I'm okay, how are you? How's the baby?"

"I'm okay, head hurts, but I split it open, so you -" She smiles, looking behind me.

I turn my head, and there up on the screen is the image of my grandbaby. There he is curled up, little fingers, little toes, his face all mushy. I can't help but squeeze Sofia's hand.

"He's perfect. Tried to say hello, but the doctors stopped it. They're gonna keep me, but you should go home."

Home. How do I tell her the house was nearly leveled? That the place she grew up in, learned to walk in is gone? "Baby, the house- I…"

"That bad?"

I nod. "There wasn't anything I could do. We were lucky to get out when we did." She starts to cry. "Baby, I'm sorry."

"I'm not crying because of the house. I'm crying because I'm thankful to still be here. Thankful, you came back for us."

"Baby, it's you and me. Forever and always. You know that." I stand up and lean into her. Kissing her head. "I'll figure it all out. I promise." She nods, and I sit, pushing the wheelchair back. I'm going to have to make some calls.

First and foremost, I need to get a hold of the insurance company. Then it's time to see what can be saved from the house. I have a promise to keep.

Chapter 25- Winnie

It's been a long couple of days. Kids don't have school. I'm waiting for someone from the insurance to come out and look everything over at the Salon. That way, we can get the insurance money to fix everything. There are so many people out of homes. I told Jarrett he could come here, but he's not left the hospital, really. I took him to get his truck, but that's been about it. I don't blame him. I'd be doing the same thing. Even with the quakes, Crew has to be at the hospital in the next six hours for surgery. The girls are with Brent and Clara. I didn't want to have to wake them up and take them with me.

When Brent said he was making room at the house for Jarrett and Sofia, boy did he. He sectioned off half the living room, putting up dividers and curtains to make a makeshift bedroom.

It's just after midnight, and I can't seem to get comfortable enough to sleep, or maybe it's just my nerves. I've checked in on Crew about a dozen or so times. He's sleeping, thankfully. Since I can't sleep, I'm packing a bag for everything we may need while we're out. Considering I have no idea how long we will be at the hospital. We're supposed to be able to come home after the surgery, but life happens, and I want to be ready.

I've not really talked to Jarrett today. Not wanting to take Crew up there and give them anything. That's the last thing Sofia needs. I pull out my phone and send him a text. If he's asleep, he'll get it when he wakes up.

WINNIE: I was thinking of you. I thought I would check-in and see how mommy and baby are doing? How's papaw? Feeling any better?

Before I can even think to put my phone away, it dings in my hand.

JARRETT: They're well, gonna be coming home today. I'm still sore, missing you.
WINNIE: Glad you all get to get out of that place. The offer to stay here is still out there, but Sofia may be uncomfortable with that.
JARRETT: Thank you, but I've already taken care of it. You know that house I was going to flip? Well, it's coming in handy now.
WINNIE: That's good you had it already and had been working on it. Anyway, you should

RESOLUTION

get some rest. You're going to have a lot on your plate once you're out of there.

I finish sending my text and start cleaning up the living room. No sense in leaving it sectioned off. My phone dings again.

JARRETT: Let me know how Crew's surgery goes. If he and the girls feel up to it, maybe you guys would like to come up for dinner tomorrow?
WINNIE: The girls are with Brent and Clara until we know what's going on, but I'll see how he's feeling and let you know.
JARRETT: Okay.
WINNIE: Goodnight.

***

I've been at the hospital since six. Crew has been in surgery since eight. It's been almost four hours, and they told me it shouldn't take more than an hour. I've not heard anything, and I'm starting to freak out. My phone is blowing up, asking how he is, and I can't answer it. I'm pacing the floor, waiting for something. I've asked for updates, and they can't give me anything. I grab my phone and drop everyone in one message together so they will shut up.

WINNIE: No updates. Crew's been in surgery for four hours. Nobody is telling me anything—Will message when I know more.
PIPER: I'm on my way.
TATUM: See you in five.

AUSTIN: Here with kids, I'm sure it's gonna be okay.
BRENTON: What do you want us to do?
BRYCE: Here for whatever you need.
JARRETT: Turn around.

I stop pacing, turning to see Jarrett. I'm in his arms in no time flat. I'm so scared, my body is shaking. Before I can stop myself, I'm crying from all the stress over the last few days and not getting any information.

"They told me it should only last an hour." I finally speak.

He winces from my grip, holding me with just one arm. The other is squashed between us. "It's okay. It may have just taken them longer than planned to put him under. It happens. They also may just not tell you anything until he's coherent and out of the transition room."

I point to a screen just across from us and show him Crew's number. "He's been in surgery for four hours. He was asleep when I left him, and they made me come back out here." I'm freaking out. I know it, but I also know there's no way to stop it until I know how my baby is.

"We'll get through it. I'm sure they will be out any moment now." Jarrett whispers. "He's a trooper and is going to be running around and making a fuss in no time."

"I sent Brad a message and never heard anything back," I say as I hear my name called.

"McCormick." Jarrett and I walk over to the doctor. "If you'll just follow me to the second room." We do, and it's like a conference room.

"Mr. McCormick, it's good to have you here. That way, you're both getting the information together."

"Um-This isn't Crew's father. Can you just tell me what happened to him, please?"

"Sorry about that. I just assumed." *You know what people get for assuming.* I think but don't speak it. "Crew had some minor complications throughout his surgery." *Complications? What the fuck?* "He doesn't handle general anesthesia well. He was vomiting, then he had quite a bit of bleeding during surgery. He's pretty swollen right now. They are working on a room for him in pediatrics. He won't be able to go home for a few days. We need to monitor him closely."

"Can we see him?" I ask, barely holding it together.

"Not quite yet. He's still in a transition room."

"Well, move him. He's twelve fucking years old." I'm getting loud, and boy, do I ever need a smoke.

"You can let her back."

I look up and see Dr. Grissom. This guy here was just a lackey, but Grissom was the actual surgeon. He approaches me. "I'm sorry I wasn't out here sooner. I wanted to make sure Crew was comfortable. Please follow me."

We're lead back to a room, and Crew is just waking up. I let go of Jarrett's hand and wrap my arms around my baby boy. I kiss him and then look him over. I can't help it; he scared me to death.

"Mom, Jarrett's a good guy." Crew says with a scratchy voice. "He loves you, but he's too chicken to say anything, and he wants you to have his baby." Crew's eyes roll around his head. "You should try it again. Maybe you'll have another boy."

I rub my hand across his cheek. "It's okay, baby. You just rest. We can talk later. Mommy loves you." With that, Crew is snoring again. I turn to look at Jarrett behind me. "Do you remember saying that?" I finally ask the man who's got a hand covering his face. I hadn't said anything because I wasn't sure about my feelings. I'm still not one hundred percent, but I do think we need to have a conversation about what was said.

"Sort of? Crew brought it up when I came out of the drug-induced fog. I-" He looks at the tile floor.

"I think it's a conversation we need to have. We need to know where each other is. You know you came out and asked me if the thing with Bryce was over, but obviously, you have or had something going on with Gabby. It's not really any of my business. I'm asking you here and now. What do you want from this?"

He sits down in the chair behind him with a heavy sigh. "The thing with Gabby and me? It's a mess. I've tried to end it a few times. She's just-she knows when my defenses are down and just when and how to strike. I've told her that it's over. It's done that I can't have that toxic relationship anymore. You- with you, *it's* different. *I'm* different. You let me help, make me

RESOLUTION

feel appreciated, validated. Like I'm not just a-" He looks at Crew. "That I'm a person to you. The baby thing, I hadn't really thought about it. I mean, not until you first brought it up, then yeah, it crossed my mind. But I know it's a deal-breaker, and I'd rather have you." He finishes making eye contact once more.

"It's not a deal-breaker, but I have a set of twins. The likely hood of me having multiples is high. Add in my age because I'm not a spring chicken. Menopause has started, and the fact I had issues with the girls. Another pregnancy could kill me, especially if it were a multiple." I say, sitting on the bed at Crew's feet, watching Jarrett.

"I'm sorry. I don't want anything to happen to you. After the quake, all I could think about was you and Sofia and your kids. I was terrified you weren't going to answer that phone."

"I won't lie. I almost didn't. I was giving a massage when the quake hit. I fell off the table and into the cabinets."

"Christ. Here I am going on about infantile bullshit, and you've been running around with a possible concussion? Did you even think about letting anyone check you out?"

"Jarrett, I'm fine. If I had a concussion, I would have fallen asleep already. I've not slept since the quake. Not that I was sleeping much before with Crew, but now there's no sleep. I lay there and stare at the ceiling."

"You need to sleep. If you don't, you are gonna crash, and if you crash, you aren't good to any of us." He gets up. "I'll make sure that they bring you a bed to the room that they move him into. You need to promise me you'll sleep."

"They have those window beds that will be fine. I can't promise I'll sleep, but I'll try." What is this *us* crap? Is he including himself? I'm so confused. I don't have any clue what we're doing. I like him a lot, and he gives me butterflies, but I don't know much more than that.

Chapter 26- Jarrett

"Daddy, really, I'm fine." Sofia pleads as I fuss at her in the living room. It's in the back of the house and closest to the kitchen in case she wants anything. The doctors say she needs rest and to keep the excitement to a minimum.

"You say that, but you've been through a trauma. We've both been through one. I mean, here I am uprooting you."

She looks around and settles into the thick padding of the couch I use for staging my houses. I have or rather *had* a storage unit full of all the furniture needed to sell the homes I work on couches, curtains, linens, just everything. The house I've owned for the last twenty-four years was a crumpled mess. There were a few salvageable rooms at the front of the house, and I was able to save a chunk of our personal belongings, but mostly it was a loss.

"I like it here." Sofia sighs, putting her feet up. "Maybe this is a good thing. Maybe you're meant to keep this place for a reason."

"Sure, just me in a five-bedroom twenty-two-acre lot."

She eyeballs me. "Maybe it doesn't have to be. Maybe if you get off your ass and take care of business, you could have some company besides me."

"What are you going on about?" I settle into the chair opposite her. I do have to admit the furniture is comfortable.

"Haven't you paid any mind to the dates? Disaster or not, you guys have been seeing each other for a month, and it's Valentine's Day, ya goof."

"So?"

"So? It's the lover's holiday. Winnie needs chocolate, flowers, a good finger bang in the bathroom while Crew's passed out."

"Sofia Marie Brooks!" I say with reddening cheeks.

"Oh, come now, daddy. I know where babies come from. That's sorta how I got here."

"Still." I shake my head. "This is not a proper conversation to have with your daughter."

"Well, it's not like you have any friends."

I glare at her.

"You don't, maybe you need to go make some, but until then, I'm going to have to lead your love life around by the nose." Her phone dings. She looks and smiles. "I'm giving Oliver the new address, so unless you want to watch me snogging him for the next few hours. I think you need to go."

"I'm not leaving you alone."

"I'm not going to be alone, Daddy. I'm going to be celebrating today."

"You need to keep the excitement down."

"I'll be fine, I promise, the first sign of a contraction, and I'll make him stop."

"Ugh! I don't want to have this conversation!" I stand up. "What would I even get her? I haven't celebrated this stupid commercial holiday since before you were born."

"Godiva, roses, and maybe jewelry? But at least Godiva and roses."

***

Stopping at the mall on the way to the hospital is a nightmare. Apparently, I'm not the only man who waits until the last possible minute to do something for his girlfriend. I brave the insane lines at the Godiva chocolate shop and manage to get a twelve-piece assortment of truffles. I beat out two other guys for the last lollipop bouquet. Being over six-foot has its advantages. I get a similar bit of stink eye from the guys in the Hallmark shop as I pick my card and a twelve-inch white plush doggy with red hearts all over him like a dalmatian. The card is a little on the cheeky side. See, it's got a picture of a wooden heart on the front that says, *This Valentine's Day lets...* and inside the card are a dozen or more sketches of screws. I think it's funny; hopefully, she will too. My last stop is in a fun little store called Tribal Art. It's a body piercing and tattoo parlor. Her bit of jewelry is not at all traditional. See, I saw to picking up a dainty sterling silver necklace with Swarovski crystals. It's a triangle made of links that travels under the clothing and attaches to her nipples. The girl behind the counter recommended it, informing me it's great for foreplay, as tugging on the chain causes epic sensations. She happened to be wearing a similar piece and flashed it to me so I could see how it looks. Once I tamed my boner, I bought the product.

With gifts in hand, I make one last stop at the toy store. Crew is probably losing his mind with nothing to really do, and I can't very well buy for one kid and not the other two. This leads me to get him a Bluetooth gaming controller for his cell phone and the girl's water bottles that they can custom color and personalize.

I arrive in the pediatrics wing just as they are passing the dinner trays. I've been getting hourly updates from Sofia, which of course, just consist of thumbs up and googly eyes. Oliver brought her dinner, apparently. I guess that makes him a better man than Fillipe already. As I approach room ten-seventy, I can hear Winnie and her pleads to Crew.

"Crew, you've got to eat *something*. Please. Just a drink? Maybe one bite? It's been over twenty-four hours. Just something, *please*."

I remember this same argument when it was Sofia. She was so swollen and miserable. I enter the room with my hands full to see it's filled with all manner of get-well stuff. Flowers, stuffed

RESOLUTION

animals, and cards. Sheesh, this kid's got a tribe. Winnie is standing over his bed, while a slender woman with dark hair sits in one of the chairs, chuckling. She all out grins, seeing me.

"Piper, would you stop? I'm already dealing with enough." Winnie looks at her friend. "What are you smiling about?"

Piper twirls her finger in my direction. "You must be Jarrett; I'm Piper. I hear you like my coffee."

"I-um-Hello," I say, looking from her to Winnie.

Winnie is biting her lip, looking at me. "She owns Sweet Caroline's. What is all that?"

Looking around for a spot to put the stuff down, I spy the daybed. Scooting by the two women and the watchful eye of the boy, I set it all down. "I realize it's all a bit late in the day, but I-well." I hold out the lollipops and card first.

"We hadn't talked about it. I just assumed you didn't celebrate it." She says, taking the stuff from me. "I didn't get you anything."

"I never knew the holiday was a reciprocal one." I smile, presenting the plush and chocolates next. "There's one more gift, but-well- open it later, okay?" I'm sure my ears are red.

Winnie sets everything down and hugs me. "You didn't have to do anything but thank you."

"Anytime," I say, looking at Crew as we break apart. "I got something for you and your sisters too." I set the control in front of him and show the bottles to Winnie and Piper.

Crew gives me a thumbs up but is starting to fall asleep. It's Piper who speaks. "Well, isn't that nice of you. Bring him for dinner. I think it's time the group gets to know him."

"I'll be in here tomorrow." Winnie answers.

"So, next Saturday then. However, I'm gonna leave you be. Things to see, people to do."

"It was nice to meet you, Piper." I nod to her as she stands.

"The pleasure is all mine, *Mister Brooks*." She practically purrs.

"Piper, keep your claws to yourself, or I will pull you bald."

"I'm just *looking*. Can't fault a woman for that." My God, these women are friends? I'd hate to hear what she thought about doing to Gabby.

With a kiss to Crew's head, Piper is out the door. Winnie is watching her the whole way.

"Sofia kicked you out, didn't she?"

"Let's say she reminded me where I needed to put my priorities." I look over at Crew, and his eyes are rolling into the top of his head. "I think it's safe to open your last gift now." I can't contain my eager smile.

"With as red as your face got, I'm excited to see. Did I bring you over to the dark side?" Winnie asks, picking up the bag. "Oh, a leash... Are you going to pull it every time I'm bad?"

I pull her toward me, the ache in my arm from the stitches is almost blinding, but I can't keep my hands to myself. "I may have to. I saw something else but thought I should discuss it with you first."

"What?" She asks curiously.

"I saw this stimulator that works long-distance, via an app," I whisper against her ear as

I inch her toward the bathroom and out of Crew's line of sight.

"Really now? Do tell more." She smiles as I pull her into the room and lock the door. Pressing her against it, I kiss her ravenously.

"You see, you stick it in your panties." My hand drops down past her waistband and into her thin cotton panties. "Letting it sit right against your clit." My thumb rubs her slowly.

"Now, I must know more." Her hands find and flip open the fly on my jeans.

"I think I remember reading that it had several vibrations and also comes with an internal vibe if you're looking to really amp up the sensations and be filled throughout the day." I finish with a grunt as I wrestle her pants down. Turning her to the wall, she bends forward, presenting her ample ass and beautifully wet pussy.

Best Valentine's Day ever.

Chapter 27- Winnie

Home. Home is one of the best places on earth. When you've spent every moment of the last four days in the hospital, then home is always the best place to be. Jarrett followed us home. Had to help get everything that everyone brought Crew. Having gotten Crew settled, I'm coming down the stairs where I can see Jarrett standing just inside the living room.

"Hey, do you want something to eat or drink?" I ask, coming off the last step.

"I think that should be my line." He says, not looking at me. "You guys went to a lot of trouble. I'm sorry, it's just that it was easier to get the other house squared away. You and the kids should really come and check it out."

RESOLUTION

"It wasn't any trouble. I just wanted her to be able to have a bed. Yeah, we will once Crew is up to it." I turn from him, heading for the kitchen.

"You've had a rough few days. Why don't you go and take a bath? I'll make some food and bring it up to you." His hand wraps my waist from behind.

"I'm okay. I need to figure out dinner. The girls will be home tonight. First time I've seen them since Thursday. They've been with Brent, and he said he was going shopping, but I don't know if he did."

"Hmm, let's see." He heads over to the cabinets. "Sofia has asked how things are at the salon. She's hoping to come in for another prenatal massage."

"They were putting in the new window today. The inside is cleaned up. A few minor fixes other than the window. Let me know what time she wants to go in, and I'll get her on someone's schedule." I say, shuffling through the mail.

"Sounds good. It looks like you got a full stock of canned veggies, fruit snacks, hand pies. I think he bought out Hostess." Jarrett laughs.

"The girls were with him. He spoils them always has." I say, sitting at the counter, opening a few bills. Not that I have the money to pay for them. The insurance only paid for the window; I had to pay out of pocket for all other repairs.

"You okay?" He asks. My face must be trying to give it away.

"Yeah, just checking out the mail. I think I'm going to grab a shower before Crew needs something. You good here for a few?"

"Yeah, do you want me to cook? I mean no sense in being idle."

"Please, anything you want is fine. The only picky eater, as you know, is the one that's barely eating." I kiss his cheek then take the mail with me out of the room.

Upstairs, I check my bank account, and it's about gone. I call Brent because, in these situations, he's the only one I trust.

"Chiquita, shouldn't you be, I don't know, passed out in bed after the week you've had? I'm bringing the girls home in like two hours. Get in the naps while you can." I can hear dishes and clanking in the background. Is he at Sweet'ums?

"I have a problem," I say, putting him on speaker as I gather my stuff for a shower.

"Okay, I may have a solution. Shoot."

"I need you to help me get another personal loan. Brad hasn't paid in the last couple of months. The insurance only paid for the window. So it's taken every penny to do the other repairs. Not leaving much to live."

I hear a hard sigh. "I want to, but I'm in a similar boat right now. My whole kitchen was wrecked by that lousy quake. Insurance is paying for the repairs, but not the loss of time or product. I'm just not sure I can help this time."

Fuck! "It's okay; I'm just sorry I even had to ask. Listen, I'm going to grab a shower before Crew wakes up. I'll see you later?"

"I'm sorry." He says softly.

"It's not your fault. If Brad would pay his fucking child support and alimony, this wouldn't be a problem."

RESOLUTION

"You need to call the lawyer, have his ass locked up, is all I'm sayin'." He's quiet a second. "I know it's a reach, but what about Bryce? He'd cut off his arm for ya if he thought it would help. Any of us would. If not us, then why not Mister Brooks?"

"No, and fuck no! He thinks I've got my shit together. I'd like to keep it that way and Bryce, and I haven't really spoken. It's been kind of weird."

"I don't know what else to suggest but let me know if there's anything else I can do to help. I love ya, kiddo, we all do." With that, he hangs up; it isn't until he does that I hear the gentle knock on my door.

"It's open," I say, wiping the tears from my face and shoving the bills under my pillow. Turning, I see Jarrett with a glass of wine and some grapes on a little platter with cheese and crackers.

"I thought I'd bring you up a little something and see if I couldn't coax you into a bath instead of the shower." His eyes are softened, and I can't help but wonder just how much he's heard.

I force a smile. "You are a very determined man. You know that?"

"I may have heard that a time or two. Honestly? It's served me rather well."

"Did you check in on Crew?" I know he should still be down, but I want to make sure.

"He was wrapped up like a burrito; I think he took a shower because there was a towel on his floor."

"That's good. At least he's starting to do stuff without being told to again. Maybe that means we're on the mend. Come on, let's go bathe together." I say, turning and knocking the bills and my pillow into the floor. I'm down trying to gather them up.

His hand crosses mine, grasping it. It's the simplest gesture, but also the kindest. "Let me help." I can't stop the pain that smacks me in the chest.

I pull back and scramble to move away from Jarrett. "No. Absolutely not going to happen." I cross my arms over my chest.

He looks down at the papers, the past due notices I've been avoiding for almost three months. "Winnie, I have the means. Let me help. I can see that your drowning. There's no way you can expect me to just stand on the shore and not dive in."

"No, Jarrett, we've barely been seeing one another a month. I'll figure it out."

"That may well be, but you're not going to sway me. Tomorrow you and I are either going down to the bank, or I'm depositing a check. One way or another, you are going to let me help." He pulls me to him across the rug. "I've just gotten you, and I won't see you or these kids suffer because you have a shitty ex-husband. If you won't take the money for free, consider it a loan. You're willing to take money from a bank that is going to hose you with interest and fees, but not from a friend? I mean, yes, we are sleeping together, but at the end of the day, I'd like to think we're friends."

RESOLUTION

"Jarrett, I can't. I can't do it. It's different with you." I say as tears fall freely. I could really use a smoke.

He pushes my hair back and kisses me. "No more arguments. No more saying no to me. I won't stand for it. You're my girl, and whatever you need, if I can provide it, I will- because that's the kind of man I am." He kisses me again. "Now, how's about that bath? Hmm, I'll rub your shoulders and wash your hair."

"*Jarrett*," I say, trying to argue my point, but he stops me, index finger to my lips.

"Not another word, the next sound I hear out of your mouth had better be a long moan, or I'm not doing something right." His determination is stronger than my resolve, and I let him get me to my feet.

Chapter 28- Jarrett

What a mess. Winnie has been hemorrhaging for a while, it would seem, and suffering in silence. She bit off more than she could chew with her salon, and while it makes enough to stay afloat, she's had to stay on top of it by taking clients to supplement the expenses of three kids and life. Her savings were depleted by Brad not paying, leaving her to let some things fall behind to unimaginable amounts. She's close to fifty grand in debt, between loans and bills.

After our talk last night, I have kept to my word. Arriving at the house as I have only, I made the demand that after she drops the girls, she comes back home. I make sure Crew is ready to leave the house by the time she returns and packing us into the truck; it's off to the bank to settle her accounts.

RESOLUTION

Winnie is quiet. I know she's not exactly thrilled with taking the money, but if she hadn't, I'd have gone to Brenton and gotten her account numbers. I'm a man that won't see those I care for suffering, and I have come to care greatly for this woman and her feisty children. So as not to embarrass her, I wrote the check off of my business account and have written it to her business account. What she does with the funds from there is up to her. We are still sitting in the truck when I decide I need to speak.

"Look at this as my making an investment. An investment in you and in your salon."

"You shouldn't have needed to do anything of the sort." She answers, looking out the window.

I finish writing the check and pass it to her. "That is a moot situation. You need it; I have it. It's done. Now take this inside and make the deposit. Then we can go get some more popsicles for Crew, and you can start writing some checks."

"Yeah, I hear you, and I'm going, but I'm paying you back." Winnie opens the door.

"That's why they call it an investment. I expect a return *eventually*." I waggle my brows.

"You're talking to the wrong girl for *that* kind of return. That's more Piper's area." Winnie answers plainly, getting out, and shutting the door.

"Why are you giving mom money?"

I look up, hearing Crew's scratchy voice. I had nearly forgotten he was in the back. "Well, the simple answer? People and Insurance industries suck. The earthquake caused a lot of damage that your mom didn't anticipate." It was mostly true. She told me she had savings she was going to dip into, but then this happened.

"She cries a lot. She doesn't think we know, but we do. We hear her. It gets really bad after dad shows up."

I nod. "Being divorced is complicated, especially with children. It will get better."

"Now that you're around? Ivy still doesn't trust you."

"I'm not saying it has anything to do with me, just with time and distance from the situation. As for your sister, well, that's up to her to decide when I'm no longer the enemy."

"Iris likes you. Ivy wants mom and dad together. Dad is never around, and when he is, it's to torture mom."

"How do you feel about that?"

"I think it's stupid, and I hate watching him hurt her. It's why it's taken her this long to find you."

I nearly smile, and before I can say another word, I spy the subject of our conversation coming out of the bank. She still looks unhappy. I wish there was a way I could put her more at ease. Take her tension away. Getting into the truck, I don't say anything. Just start us up.

"Mom?"

"Yeah, Crew?" Winnie answers.

"Why don't you ever go on dates with Jarrett or stay the night with him? Isn't that what couples your age do?"

RESOLUTION

I can't help but snicker a tad as Winnie answers. "We've had dates. Just because you don't know about them doesn't mean it hasn't happened."

"Have you had sex?"

"Crew Carter McCormick! Where do you get off asking a question like that?"

"I have a right to know if you're going to be having his baby."

"Crew, just because a couple has sex doesn't mean they are going to have babies. The world has come a long way in the realms of birth control, as you should be learning in school by now." I answer plainly.

"But you asked her to have your baby?"

I look at Winnie, who's got her hands sprawled over her face, then I glance at Crew in the mirror. He's staring intently. I don't know how to answer that. "The head and the heart don't always go at the same speeds. While I was under the influence of a lot of drugs, one spoke louder than the other of thoughts entertained but not fully thought through. Does that make sense to you?"

"You were thinking with your *penis*?"

"Oh, my God! Crew go back to not talking." Winnie's face is blood red.

Chuckling. "No, no, for once, I was not."

"You have to use your penis to get a baby."

"Yes, but you also have to have a serious conversation and be on the same page about what you want to do once that baby is conceived. Your mom and I have had that conversation, and as of right now, babies are not on the menu of our relationship. The three of you, my daughter, and my soon to be grandson, are more than enough."

"Dude, how *old* are you? Are you too old for mom? She's not old enough to be a grandma yet."

"Old enough to know better and young enough to snag a hottie like your mom," I smirk. "Enough already. If you can flap your yap like this, you are *so* ready to go back to school."

"It was quiet in here, and you talked to me while mom was in the bank about dad." Crew says, and if looks could kill, Winnie would strike me dead.

Chapter 29-Winnie

Getting home after the bank was eventful. We barely got Crew to shut up. He kept talking about things I'd much rather not, especially not with my almost thirteen year old. The fact that I'm now sitting in the office with Jarrett, either cutting checks or paying online all the bills I owe, is about to send me into a full-blown panic attack. What is he going to expect from me now? Is he going to hold this over my head? Is he going to use it against me? It's what Brad would have done. When I had to ask for money, he always held it over my head and against me. There were even a few times where he would say since he paid for whatever that I'd have to give him head or spread my legs. So again, I have to ask myself, what is Jarrett going to expect from me?

Waiting on my computer to load, I try to rub the migraine that is forming away.

"Do you keep any of those essential oils in the house? Maybe some tea tree would help with your head? I'd be happy to go grab it." He gently grasps my shoulder.

"No, I don't. I'll be fine. It's something I just have to work through. I'll be okay after a while. Thanks away."

He sighs. "Do you want me to go make lunch? Or would you rather I go and leave you to this?" He stands up. "It's been a while since it's just been you and your place to just have some space. Maybe that's what you need."

"No, I need to know what you want. What do expect from me? Is this going to be held over my head because you thought I had my shit together, and I didn't?" I have to go under the desk to get away from him as I have an L shaped desk.

"Want from you?" He looks at me, confused. "I didn't do this for some kind of *leverage* if that's what you're insinuating. What kind of man-no person do you take me for? I gave you this money because you need it and I have it to give. For fuck's sake, Winnie, I don't care if you even pay it back. All I want is for you to be able to breathe a little easier. Not have to worry if that piece of shit ex of yours is gonna hold out another month out of spite and do for yourself and the kids without worry. Why? Because that's what you do for the people, you care about. You take care of them. Without questions, or motives, or expectations of returns. You do it because you can because it's the right thing to do and because actions speak far louder than words ever could." Jarrett walks toward the door. "Now, if you really in your heart think that I'm in this for anything other than you and your happiness, say the word, and I'll go because I won't have you looking at me like you have all day. Acting like I'm going to drop some proverbial shoe. When all I want to do is try to love you."

I twirl one of the kid's chairs and sit down before my legs give out on me. "It's all I know. The guy I'm with holds it over my head or uses it against me. The same thing goes for my parents. I hate taking money from people for that reason. It's why Brent just co-signs on a loan, but you wouldn't do that." I run my fingers under my eyes to wipe away the mascara that I know is running.

"The bank would have charged you a crazy amount of interest. Just look at me as the bank of Jarrett, interest-free, and happy to make any adjustments you may need. Still, I'm not doing this as some way of trying to gain control over you or your business. Winnie, I'm not that person. I just wish you could see that." Jarrett looks at the ground.

"I know, I'm sorry. Maybe it's best if we, I don't know, take a break until I can work through my head. I love having you around, but when you're around, I think about one thing and one thing only." I say, wrapping my arms around myself.

Without looking up, he nods, his hand on the doorknob. "I understand. I don't like it, but I understand. Good-bye, Winnie." He finishes in a whisper before walking out the door.

He doesn't even get the door shut before I start sobbing. I'm a mess, and I know it. I can't expect anyone to deal with it if I can't. I try to pull myself together as I grab my phone and send a message.

WINNIE: Can someone pick up the kids today?
TATUM: I thought Jarrett was staying with Crew?
WINNIE: Things came up.
PIPER: You're an idiot. She ran him off!
TATUM: Winnie, he was good for you.
WINNIE: I'm fucked up, okay? I have issues.
BRENTON: We aren't discussing those. We'd be here all day. I'll get the girls. You better keep your therapy appointments.
WINNIE: I can't. I'll have to look at what I did every time. Then I'll just start crying again. I let myself push him away because I care too much.
PIPER: You're a chicken shit.
WINNIE: Yeah, I know I am.
PIPER: Go to him and tell him you love him. It was all over your damn face at the hospital. The both of yours.
WINNIE: I've already fucked it up. I accused him of being like Brad.
TATUM: Are you fucking kidding me? He's nothing like Brad.
BRYCE: Ain't nothing in this world can't be fixed by a little honesty. If you love him. Tell him.

RESOLUTION

WINNIE: I can't. I've already hurt him. I did to him what Brad always did to me. I'm so stupid.
BRENTON: Stop telling us and go tell him!
AUSTIN: Um, guys- She just did. Jarrett is IN THIS CHAT!

I toss my phone across the room like it just shocked me. I look up as the door opens, not sure if I want it to be Jarrett or not. I'm left to the pit in my stomach as I see Crew.

"Mom, are you okay? It sounded like something smashed." Crew asks with sad eyes.

"My phone slipped from my hand." I lie. Looking at it on the shelf under the command center. It knocked a couple of clipboards down. Crew walks over to where my phone is and picks it up, typing something. "Hey, don't do that."

"Why not? You've lost your mind. Jarrett was good to you and us, and you let him walk out the door."

"Crew, you don't know what you're talking about."

"You asked him to leave. Do you love him? I don't want to go back to *this* you. You actually smiled when you started talking to him. Now we're back to crying. I say no."

"Crew give me my phone. This is adult stuff." I say, trying to get up and trip over the leg, smacking my face on the floor.

"Are you done lying to yourself? Ready to admit you love Jarrett?"

"Fine Crew, I made a mistake. I love Jarrett, and I pushed him away. Is that what you want to hear?"

"I think that will do it."

"Can I have my phone now?" After typing a few more things, he gives me my phone. I look and see he's sent a video. "You've got to be kidding me!"

Chapter 30-Jarrett

Bombarded. Bells, dings, and rings. That's what my phone is doing on the dashboard of my truck. Having taken on a life of its own just moments after I walked out Winnie's front door. She asked me to leave, and though it ripped my heart out, I did as she asked. Of course, Crew spotted me on the way out and begged me not to go, making it all the worse. Here I am, at the end of her driveway with such a pain in my chest that I can't move. There was a video that came through of Winnie. She's a mess too. She says she loves me and all other manners of things, but I just- I can't move. I can't breathe, my vision is blurred, and my mouth is dry. Everything is-is just...

***

"Jarrett, wake up. Talk to me. Please. Crew! Are they on their way? Dear God! Jarrett, wake up." Winnie sounds frantic. *Why does Winnie sound frantic?* I can feel her on me, her hands on my stomach, pressing down. I feel like I'm gonna puke.

My eyes open with a pained squint. "Winnie? What are you doing? Why are you on top of me?"

"Jarrett? Are you okay? How many fingers am I holding up?" She asks, holding up three fingers.

I grasp her hand. "It's not my vision that's impaired," I mutter, wiggling, trying to get her off of me. "I'm fine now. Not sure what that was, but it's passed."

"Quit moving. The EMT is on the way. Does your chest hurt? Can you breathe, okay?"

"My heart is shattered, and I could breathe better without the extra hundred and twenty pounds on what's left of my guts," I grunt, not looking at her.

"Dammit, Jarrett, you passed out. It had to be from *something*." She says, grasping my face to make me look at her. She can turn my head, but she cannot control my eyes, which I cast downward. If I look at her and see anything in her eyes, I won't be able to take it. She's broken me and doesn't even recognize her own work.

"Please get off of me."

"Fine, I just want to make sure you're okay. You don't just pass out for nothing." She says as she starts to move and falls into the floorboard. "Fuck." She cries out.

I look down and watch as she pulls the business end of a Phillips head screwdriver from her calf. "For fuck's sake." I rub my chest as it's still aching.

Winnie scoots, trying to get out of the truck. "I'll pay for your truck to be cleaned. I'm sorry. I just wanted to make sure you were okay." She says, climbing out of the truck.

"Winnie?" I call after her. She's bleeding like a stuck piggy. "You need to have that looked at, and you need a tetanus shot. That driver was covered in muck." I go to get out of the truck, and as soon as my feet hit the ground, my knees buckle, and down I go. *Fuck.*

"You're the one that needs to be seen. You can't even stand." Winnie turns back to me but has to use the truck to stay standing.

"Pot, meet kettle," I say, feeling that heaviness in my chest return as I watch her and hear the sirens approaching. Crew is just watching us with the phone in his hands.

"I'm not arguing with you. I don't want to-" Winnie's speaking when her leg finally gives and can't hold her weight anymore. "Crew, get your shoes on, and come."

"I'm good. Piper is on her way to stay with me." Crew hollers back, amused.

"Damn it, Crew, get off my phone and bring it and my purse to me."

Crew walks over to Winnie and holds her stuff over her head. "Tell him how you feel."

"It doesn't matter. Give me my stuff."

"Tell Jarrett how you feel about him." Crew says again.

"Kid- leave it. She may *love* me, but she doesn't *want* me. Wanting me is a liability." I press into my ribs, hoping it will stop the pain that just won't go away.

"You don't get to speak. You were too chicken to tell her the truth too."

I drop my head. He's right, after all. I couldn't just tell her, but how do you declare something like that after only a month of knowing someone? That's crazy, isn't it? How do I know it isn't just the circumstances that have made me feel like this? That this isn't just convenience? Here we go again. My heart and head are pounding. The paramedics are here. One has gone to Winnie. The other is talking to me. Accessing my situation. Taking my blood pressure, listening to my heart, my lungs.

I'm watching them taking care of her, making sure she's going to be okay. "Quit fussing over me. My leg will be fine. Jarrett is the one that passed out." Winnie complains.

"Is he your husband, ma'am?" The paramedic asks her.

"No, I fucked that up. I told him to leave even when I shouldn't have."

"Was this a domestic disturbance?"

"Are you fucking delusional? Do you see his size? Domestic disturbance? What do you think I could do to him?"

"You've been stabbed, *ma'am*."

"I fell on fucking a screwdriver. Stitch it up, give me the God damned tetanus shot, and worry about *him*."

"He's in excellent care."

"He's holding his fucking chest. How good could that be?"

"For someone that says it doesn't matter, you're both awfully worried about the other one." Crew spouts.

"Shut up, Crew."

They've silenced me with an oxygen mask, telling me to breathe. I'm having an anxiety attack. They are now giving me something to calm me down before transporting me to the hospital for further testing. They roll up a gurney and make me get on as I watch them tend to Winnie further. A second gurney is rolled out as Piper's mustang pulls up alongside my truck.

They're strapping me down as she gets out and hurries over to Crew and Winnie.

"Crew, did you stab your mother so that they both have to go to the hospital?"

"No! They were in the truck rolling around. I figured they were doing something I really didn't want to see."

"We're not together, Crew. I fucked that up. Can you give me my stuff and just go inside now?"

"As soon as you admit it."

"Admit what?"

"That you love him."

"Christ! I love him, and it scares me to death. Because the last man I loved hurt me so bad I didn't think I would recover. So instead of taking the chance of getting hurt again, I pushed him away." Winnie shouts as they put her on the gurney.

I'm lifted into the ambulance and locked into one side. Everything hurts. I feel like I'm going to die right here. I fight against the straps.

"Easy there, Mister Brooks, you're gonna hurt yourself." One of the EMT's says her hand on my shoulder, trying to keep me down.

"Lift me up, you idiot!" I shout from under the mask. "I need to get to her. I've been so stupid." I pant. The drugs they gave me are starting to work. I can feel my body getting heavy. Through blurry eyes, I see them lifting her in beside me. Locking her in with me. She's upright, facing me, her hands in her lap. She's still crying as they hook her up to stuff. I struggle even as my vision blurs again. I manage to break my arm free, and sure I've torn my stitches, I reach out.

"Winnie?"

She looks in my direction seeing my hand. She lets her fingers touch mine. "Let them take care of you. They know what to do." She says even through the crying.

I stretch enough that I get a grab of her hand. "I love you."

Chapter 31-Winnie

He said he loved me, but then he passed out. Was it him, or was it the drugs? That last time he said anything like this, it was when he had drugs too. It was easy. They cleaned me up, patched my leg, and then gave me a shot in my arm. Jarrett? He's still back in a room, and the idiots in this place won't give me any information.

"We came in on the same fucking ambulance," I growl, trying to get back to see him. I need to know if he meant it.

"I'm sorry, ma'am, only the family is allowed information."

"Coming in together should amount for something!"

"If you don't go sit down and wait for him to come out, then I will have to call security."

"Winnie!" I turn, hearing Sofie's voice. She's followed by a tall blonde guy, and Christ, she's popped. there's no denying there's a baby on board now. "Where's my dad?"

"They won't let me see him or give me any information," I say, trying to calm myself. She pulls me into a hug.

"I got you." She turns and looks at the Charge Nurse. "I'm Sofia Brooks-Guteriez. My father is Jarrett Brooks. His birthday is April twenty-sixth, seventy-seven. Now you are gonna tell my friend and me here where he is, or I'm going to drop this baby right here on your floor? If I do that, I'm then going to take your computer and shove it so far up your ass that my birth will seem like a fucking dream. Do I make myself abundantly clear?" She says this so calmly that I'm left to wonder if threats are a specialty of hers.

"Please don't drop the baby. Your dad would not like that." I say to Sofia, then look at the nurse. "Open the fucking door."

"Bed seven." She says, holding name tags out, and I yank them from her hand before running down the hall and back into the rooms.

Jarrett's sitting up in bed when I come through the curtain and straight to him. "Are you okay? Have they said anything?" I fuss, looking him over.

Grabbing me, he kisses me. "You almost killed me." He whispers millimeters from my lips. "Thinking I was never going to be near you again literally tried to break my heart."

RESOLUTION

"I'm so sorry. I would have been back here sooner, but the nurse wouldn't let me. I looked for you on my way out but couldn't find you then either. Christ. I'm so stupid. Please don't be mad at me." Tears fall down my face.

"Stop. Stop crying. I can't take more of that." He wipes at my cheek. "They said it was a severe anxiety attack which caused the palpations, which snowballed. I'm going to be fine. They did an echo and EKG. It was all good. How's your leg?"

I climb into the bed and straddle him. "It's just a few stitches. You scared me to death. I thought you had a heart attack or something." I kiss him again.

"So did I." He wraps his good arm around me. "I'm sorry it took thinking I was dying to tell you, I love you."

"I'm sorry for pushing you away. I shouldn't have done it." I hug myself to him.

"Could you two at least wait for a room with a door and maybe some walls?" Sofie's voice breaks in. "Sheesh. Now, will someone tell me what the fuck happened?"

"I was stupid. I caught feelings and tried to push your dad away." I say, never letting my eyes sway from his. "It's the last thing I could possibly want. I love him, you see, and I'm kind of hoping you are okay with that because I don't think I could ever live without your dad in my life."

"Uh-huh. So you're moving in then?" Sofia says plainly. "Sounds good."

"We haven't talked about that yet." I watch Jarrett's expression. He lifts his brows as if to say, why not. "Sofia doesn't need to be around Crew right now. We'd have to soundproof rooms. The last thing they need is to hear her or us. You're serious? Is there even enough room?"

"Sofia has taken over the basement rooms since we've moved in. This way, Oliver can come and go. So that covers that. Then I have another three rooms besides mine, not to mention rooms that can be modified or changed if ever needed." He squeezes me. "I know it's a lot, and it's fast, but it would solve a lot of problems, and I would like very much to wake up with you in my arms."

"What about my house? I still owe on it?" I ask, even though he's going to say something to discontinue any thoughts I may be having."

"I'll buy it. Renovate it and sell it." He smiles. "It's what I do."

"You're crazy. You know that?"

"A brush with death just brings the priorities into perspective." He kisses me, and I feel his priorities all right.

"Okay, I'm obviously not needed here. I'm going home. Winnie, it was nice seeing you."

"Thanks for getting me back." I wave without looking at her. "I love you and what I'm feeling, but um, right here might not be the right place. Plus, if we're doing this, we need to break it to the kids."

"Then we'd had better get me discharged, huh?"

***

My house is quiet, and that's just something that doesn't ever happen with three kids. The kids are on the couch, with Jarrett and I sitting on the chairs in front of them. The only thing separating us is the coffee table. We decided it would be easier to just tell them instead of talking around it.

"Do we get to take our things?" Iris asks.

"Yes, of course, you do," I answer.

"I want to go live with dad," Ivy says, crossing her arms over her chest.

"Ivy, we've talked about this. You live with me, and your dad gets visitation."

"I bet you won't even tell him where we'll be living." She spouts.

"Dad doesn't care about us anyway. God!" Crew says, getting up and moving away from Ivy.

"Do we get to pick out a house together, or does Jarrett already have one?" Iris asks, trying to stop the fight that we all know is coming.

"He has a home," I say, putting my hand in his. "You all get your own rooms. Crew would have his own bathroom, but you two would share one."

"Look, it won't happen tomorrow. I want you to be happy with your spaces, so we'll spend time fixing up your rooms together. Painting, and whatever else you want. I have space for your gaming stuff from downstairs, so you don't have to give any of that up either. Plus, I've got a pool and swings. I live within walking distance of a park, and Brighton beach isn't far away either." Jarrett tries to sweeten the prospect.

"Do we have to change schools?" Crew asks.

"I don't think so. I don't want you to have to lose your friends, and I'll still be doing the carpool, so that helps."

"What are you going to do with the other stuff?" Iris asks.

"What stuff, sweetheart?"

"Our furniture and outdoor stuff?"

"Well?" I say, not sure how to answer that.

"I have a lot of that stuff, but I'm sure we can mix it up, keep some of mine, keep some of yours. How's that sound? My yard is large, so if you have favorite things, I'm sure there's room enough." Jarrett smiles.

"Are you two going to have babies and forget us?" Iris asks seriously.

"I could never forget any of you ever. As for babies, I think right now we're good with what we've got. You three keep me plenty busy."

Jarrett laughs. "Babies. There will be one. My daughter Sofie is having a little boy soon. She's staying with us too. So that will make you guys honorary aunties and an uncle if that interests you. Let's call him a test run."

"A test run?" I ask him. He shrugs at me.

"Are you getting married or just living in sin?" Ivy says disdainfully.

"Honestly, we haven't talked about that, but as soon as we know, you will know. Okay?"

"So, you're going to hell." Ivy smarts.

"Ivy Kathleen, I've heard about enough of your mouth. I don't want to hear another word if you can't be polite."

"Will I still be able to have a boy, girl party for my birthday?" Crew asks.

RESOLUTION

"Do you really think that's wise?" I raise a brow.

"Yeah?" Crew questions.

"Your mom and I will talk about it. I have the space, and so long as we're not talking about a sleepover, I think it can be arranged." Jarrett nods, standing up. "Now, it's been a long day. Why don't we order some pizza and try to unwind from the day's excitement?"

"What's a boy, girl party? Boys and girls always come to our parties?" Iris asks.

"It's when they kiss and experiment on each other," Ivy says.

"You lie."

"No, I didn't. Ask Crew. He's the one that told me."

Crew holds his hands up. "I never said anything like that. I swear."

"We are *not* having this conversation. *Not* right now, *not* tonight." I practically cry.

Jarrett pulls me up to stand. "Come on, let's just go order dinner." He hugs me, then whispers in my ear. "Then, after they go to bed, we can have our own boy, girl party."

Chapter 32-Jarrett

The weekend comes, and with it, the Honey-do list. See, I'm involved with a woman that is partial to the color blue. So I am, therefore, on the hunt for gallons of variations of that core color. Crew's room is a shade of cobalt, and what was my dining room with the addition of the pocket doors now will become her office, which is getting a coat of Tiffany blue.

The girls are looking at paint chips while I pull the base gallons we are going to need. Fortunately, the whole house is already primer white.

"Can I have a multi-colored room?" Iris asks me.

I look at Winnie, "So long as you're not huffing the paint, I don't care what color you paint your rooms."

RESOLUTION

"I want lime green, pink, and aqua!"

"Like stripes? Flowers? One wall of each or stenciling stuff?" I quirk a brow.

She looks at me with wide eyes. "Like an aqua ceiling with clouds and a pink wall with lime decorations. I saw a cool mirror with lime and polka dots. Then there were these hanging lights over there that are pink, and I saw a rug too!"

I laugh. "Alright. sounds like you've got it figured out." I look at Ivy, who's a bit further down the aisle with a couple of chips in her hand. "Have you found anything, Ivy?"

Ivy hands the paint chips to Winnie. "No! Absolutely not happening. This is crazy. We are not doing a red and black bedroom."

"Why not? Jarrett said we could have what we want. That's what I want!" She stomps her foot.

Before Winnie can react, I take her by the elbow, getting her attention. She looks at me like she's gonna eat me.

"I did say that" I say softly.

"*You* said that *I* didn't." Winnie counters me.

"Compromise? One red wall, black lacquer trim, bedding on color rotations with black trimmings. Furniture within reason and no black flooring."

"I don't like it. I don't think it's a good idea."

"I get it; she's your little girl." I turn her from the kids as I speak, my finger tracing her neckline. "But therein lies the reasoning." I tug on the chain connected where none can see, but she can feel. "One of the apples was bound to stay near the tree." I kiss her a little more roughly than the audience should allow, but I needed to make my point and get Ivy her red room.

"You're not playing fair." She whimpers.

I tug a little harder. "So is that a *yes*?"

"Do I have a choice?" She asks as her fingers dig into my sides.

"Sure, if you like to see looks of disappointment rather than pleasure." I pull up, changing the sensation, I'm sure.

"I like seeing your pleasure."

"Let me stay over tonight."

"Come with me tonight?"

"If you like." I smile, kissing her once more before letting her go.

"Fine, give her the room. I'm going to message Brent and tell him to make room for one more."

"You won't regret it." I look over at Ivy, who's chattering with Iris. "We've got a compromise for you. Take it or leave it."

She looks at me with her brow quirked before looking at her mother and sticking out her tongue. "Take it."

***

Since I was invited to dinner, Winnie and I parted ways after picking up everything for the house. I drop her and the kids off at her place before zipping back to mine to pull myself together. I pack a bag with a change of clothes and other needed items, then nice and clean, I haul ass back to Winnie. Knocking on the door, I wait, rather impatiently, I might add. Or is it more nervously? We've had our fair share of lunches, but this is our first adult dinner. The first time I'm meeting the group. I've met the majority at some point—Piper at the hospital and the house. Tatum at the salon, and of course, Brenton and I have a bit of history from employing Sofia for a time. My concern is Bryce and Austin. The other men of the group. Are they going to be okay? Or are they going to be thorns in my side? I love Winnie, but I don't feel I should have to prove that love repeatedly forever to please them. I know I have hoops to jump through, and that is fine. But this tiger will only jump for so long.

The door opens, and its Crew. "Come on, she's taking *forever* tonight."

I smile, brandishing my bouquet of orange roses with baby's breath. "Thank you." I step inside and head for the living room to wait for her. Like a real date should.

"She's been getting ready since she got home! What did you tell her?" Crew complains, falling against the couch.

"Not a thing." I chuckle. "Where are your sisters?"

"Packing their closets to take to Austin's."

"Ah, and you? You don't pack a bag?"

"It's Saturday. I'm already done. I was done before you all left today."

"A man who prepares that's a sign of good things."

"Speaking of good things. We need to get something straight."

I quirk a brow at him.

"You will *not* be asking her to marry you without us there. *I* should be asked first."

"I'll do you one better. Should the time come, I'll take the three of you with me to pick the ring. How does that sound?" I walk over to him extending my hand.

He gives a good hard shake. "Nothing too big she's got tiny hands."

"Noted." I hold his little hand firm. "And while we're on the subject of agreements. *You* will not bring girls into my house for the purpose of sexual relations. Is that understood?"

"What happened to it being our house?" He counters just like his mother would.

"Oh, it is our house, but if your mother catches you with a girl, it's my ass. So do we have an understanding?"

"I'm not going to stay a virgin forever, so I can't promise to *never* have sex under your roof. Isn't that what Sofia is doing?"

"Sofia is twenty-five and-" I stop hearing Winnie on the stairs. "To be continued?" I say, letting his hand go and turning my attention to the hallway. I can't believe a twelve-year-old is besting me. I hear the click-clack of heels on the hardwood floor. That's a new sound. Licking my lips, I anticipate her appearance. What will it be? Capris and a little tank? Skinny jeans and a button-down or possibly a skirt?

"Where is everyone? I thought I heard the door?" Her voice proceeds her as she appears from the darkened hall. My eyes cast over her. She took the time to change her polish color. Her toes are black wrapped in these strappy umber colored heels. Her bare legs look silky smooth and perfectly kissable. Her body is covered in a dark brown dress that cuts above mid-thigh, with suede cut-ins and a zipper front going up to a deep V-neckline with little capped sleeves. Her dark hair is down, and her lips have just a hint of peach gloss.

"Ouch," I mumble, biting my lip. Not realizing I had pulled it into my mouth as I took her in.

Winnie pulls her lip into her mouth, failing to hide a smile, but it's Crew who speaks. "Wow, mom, you look nice."

"Thanks, baby, wanna go grab your sisters so we can go? We're already running late."

"Okay." Crew glances at me with a laugh.

Winnie doesn't speak until he's going up the stairs. "You look nice."

I'd pulled out a casual blazer and, pairing it with a decent dress shirt and jeans, left my usual baseball cap at home. "Not nearly as nice as you." I hold out the roses. "For you."

"More roses? What did I do to deserve these?" She smells them. "We should put them in water." Turning away, she heads for the kitchen with me right behind. Like any man, my eyes zero in on what's before me. Her ripe round, swaying ass. Fuck me, not a seam or crease under that dress, so either she's got lycra to the thigh, or she's not wearing any panties. I'm determined to find out, just as we get into the kitchen, and I get behind her. I'm foiled by the sound of the twin's voices.

Cocked blocked.

"Are we ready to go? Echo is waiting for me, and Ashton has friends over tonight."

"What friends?" Winnie asks.

"Boys from the soccer team," Ivy says, walking in the room. She's in a damn mini skirt, or at least that's what it looks like with her long legs. "Kris asked me to be his girlfriend."

I look at Winnie, concerned. She pats my chest. "Calm down, Papa Bear. It's normal. Ivy, will you tell Jarrett where your dates are so he will quit freaking out."

"Lunch in the cafeteria and on the playground." Iris answers coming into the room with a nice little dress on and lip gloss.

If Winnie isn't stressing, I can't. I have to remember this is a different time. These are different girls. They are not Sofia. Christ don't let them be like Sofia was! I nod. "Just don't come home with mono like your brother. Date smarter than that," I say calmly.

"Eww! I'm not kissing boys until I'm thirty." Iris answers.

"I was thinking more like sixteen," Ivy responds to her sister.

"I'll take what I can get. Now let's get going. We ready?" I look to Winnie.

"Crew's upstairs, spiking his hair. Cassi is going to be there until ten. Means more kissing. Yuck!" Iris sticks out her tongue.

"Maybe we should stay home," Winnie says.

"Nope, you put on a pretty dress. We're going out.- CREW! Ass down here now!" I holler after him. "We are leaving!"

RESOLUTION

"I'm changing. I can't wear my spiderman boxers."
"BOY!"

Chapter 33-Winnie

Pulling up to Sweet'ums, I'm a ball of nerves. Not because I'm with Jarrett and he's accompanying me to dinner with my friends. No, it's because my almost thirteen year old and all his hormones is with his girlfriend right now. Jarrett gets out then helps me.

"One drink, then we have to go back and get the kids."

Jarrett squeezes my hand. "Winnie, you and me, we are not bailing on our first night out together. The kids are going to be okay. As for Crew, I may have set twenty or twenty-five different alarms on his phone to go off randomly all night. Making it impossible for him to hit any sort of groove." I grin at her.

"I'm not ready to be a grandma because my thirteen-year-old has a kid." I look up at Jarrett.

RESOLUTION

"You need to trust him. Trust that he's smarter than you give him credit for. Now, if you're going to wring your hands tonight, wring them over me being thrown to the lions. Have you told them we're shacking up yet?"

"Brent and Piper know." I smile at him.

"So for the rest, I'm just being thrown under the bus? Got it." He pulls me along, and we're spotted before I can negotiate a crafty escape.

"Let's get a drink," I say, stopping at the bar where I spot Brenton. "I need something tall and strong," I call over the bar.

"You want that from Long Island?" Brenton snickers turning to face us. "Well, lookie here ain't we all gussied up, what's the occasion?"

"Apparently, I'm feeding Jarrett to the lions, but really it's our first night out together. Oh, and let's not forget Crew is going to make me a grandma tonight. Did you know Austin was letting kids come to his house?" I look at Brenton. "Oh, my bad. Brenton Sweet, Jarret Brooks, my *boyfriend*. Not that you two don't know one another, but ya know formalities and all that jazz."

Jarrett graciously reaches across the bar and shakes Brenton's hand. "Good to see you."

"You too. How's Sofia?"

"Pregnant, separated, living back home. You know the usual." He laughs.

"Wow, I didn't realize it."

"It's fine; she's happy and healthy. So why don't you mix Winnie up her drink, then you can pass me a beer and get your ass out here because

I'm gonna need all the buffers I can get with this crowd."

"You aren't gonna need a buffer. You may need a shield to keep them off your sword, though. Between this one and Piper, Lord knows it's gonna be a night of innuendo, and nip slips galore!"

Jarrett looks at me, puzzled. "You gonna turn me out, baby?"

"Baby is what I call Crew. Find a new name. Besides, you were worried. Now you don't have to be." She winks at me taking her drink. "We'll see you over there, Brent."

Piper is up, waving at us. *99 Problems* by Hugo comes over the speakers, and we sing it at the same time as we make our way to the table. I put my drink down.

"I wish I could say a bitch ain't one." I laugh. I start ticking everyone off. "Austin Doyle, Bryce Blackmon, and you know Tatum Greathouse and Piper O'Reilly. This is Jarrett Brooks, my boyfriend."

Austin smiles. Next to him is a pair of crutches. "I'd stand, but that earthquake temporarily disabled me." He leans forward, and Jarrett reaches across the table to shake his hand, just as Bryce stands. This was the one I've worried about from the start.

"Good to finally meet you. We were starting to think she was going to keep you tied up somewhere forever." He smirks.

"Not likely, as we haven't settled on our safe word just yet. I've been thinking Cantaloupe. What do you think?" He looks at me.

"I think Meatloaf would be better," I answer seriously and then take a drink.

Jarrett looks at me with an eyebrow raise.

"Meatloaf? Get it, because she'd do anything for love, but she won't do that?" Brenton snickers.

Jarrett nods, pulling out my chair before sitting down himself.

"So, Austin, what's with the party at your place?" I ask. "Trying to make me a grandma?"

"It's just a couple of the boys from the soccer team, Cassi, and a couple of Clara's girlfriends from school. Clara promised me no shenanigans, and everyone would be gone by ten, except for Alex. her friend, who was going to the mall with her tomorrow."

"Kris asked Iris to be his girlfriend, and Cassi gave Crew mono just FYI."

"Now, you tell me!" Austin shakes his head. "For fuck's sake, Win, you gotta keep me more up to date on this shit. I thought Cassi was seeing Ashton."

"She's thirteen! All I'm saying is if Crew shows symptoms again, he's staying with you. I don't have time with packing to move."

All uninformed eyes roll to me.

"Move?" It is damn near-unanimous.

"We're moving in with Jarrett."

All eyes now sail to him.

He smiles, sipping his beer. "Yes?"

"Are you sure about this? You just started dating." Tatum is the first to speak up.

"Is this because of Brad coming back around?" Bryce asks, his brow crinkled in concern. "We can always take care of that, you know?"

"Why you guys hating on this? If they wanna be, let 'um be." Austin breaks in. "How are the kiddos taking it?"

"Crew and Iris are fine. Ivy is getting a red and black room." I answer honestly, slipping my hand into Jarrett's.

"Has he even met your parents?"

"No, and hopefully will never have to." Again another honest answer. Jarrett's hand tightens around mine.

"This was the most irrationally rational choice we could make. We talk every day. Since Crew got sick, I've been around all the time. Since my other home was destroyed by the quake, I've moved into a house far too large for just me and Sofia, so I've invited Winnie and the kids to be with us. Where I believe we and they can not only live well but thrive. It may be fast to some of you, but when love hits, it hits, and this is a grand slam."

"This would be why I've been keeping him to myself. He's so smart and sweet and kind." I lay my head against Jarrett's arm. "Anywho, we're going to start painting next week. We'd like to have it done by Crew's birthday."

"I can send the boys to help if you need it," Piper says.

"I know we'll need help with the furniture."

"That would be great, thank you." Jarrett nods. "I'm not much help with the stitches."

"I'll send Dante over too. He's good for painting ceilings." Bryce smiles.

RESOLUTION

I snort a laugh remembering the first time I talked to Jarrett on the phone, Dante was at the house, and he thought I was with someone. It's also the same time he hung up on me. I look at Jarrett and wink.

"Love looks good on you, Win," Piper says far too loud and then. "Shots!"

***

A few hours later and we're all on our way to drunk. Piper pulls me from my chair to dance with me as Christina Aguilera's *Come on over Baby* comes through the speakers. The best thing about Saturday's at Sweet'ums you get a mix of new and old music. Piper racks her hands down my body as I shake my ass. She lets go of me, and I grab Jarrett's hand pulling him to me.

"I warn you; I white boy dance." He laughs. Grabbing my ass, pressing unbeknownst to him on the little something I have hidden under my dress as a surprise. I'm currently wearing a jeweled butt plug. It not only keeps me aroused all night but also serves as a way to tease him once he strips me later.

"Can I tell you a secret?" I ask, licking my lips.

His hand slides up to the small of my back as he pulls me into him. "I'm all ears."

"I'm so wet, I'm starting to drip."

"You wanna go home?" He asks, bending down and kissing me.

"I want you to fuck me long and hard."

"Definitely arrangeable." He says from low in his chest, pressing against me. I can feel his hardening cock as he backs us off the dance floor. "You grab your purse. I'll call the Uber."

"Don't let him go down. I want to play on the way home." I say, cupping him in my hand.

He groans, pulling from me headed for the doors.

Chapter 34-Jarrett

One-track mind. That's me right now as I bounce from foot to foot outside Sweet'ums. All I want to do is get my hands on Winnie. Her teases in the bar were enough to rile me up worse than the night she called me from here. Every set of heels on the pavement behind me has my cock twitching thinking it's her. That dress unzips in the front. I can have her naked and moaning almost instantly. Devouring her breasts, her mouth. I jump as arms wrap around me, so caught up in my building fantasy. I didn't hear her approach.

"You okay there?" Winnie's voice fills my ears. I pull her to my front and crush her against me for a hungry kiss.

"The Uber is going to be at least half an hour more," I growl against her throat, nipping at her flesh.

"Whatever will we do to pass the time?" Winnie asks as her hands go up into my shirt.

I bury my face in her neck, taking in her scent, something sorta fruity, a little bit floral. "What have you got in mind?" I groan.

"There's a place we used to smoke on the side where nobody goes."

"Get a room." Some guy barks as he walks by.

I start to laugh, grabbing her by the hand. "Show me."

She pulls me along with her to the dark alley. "We should be good right here," Winnie says, pulling my face down to meet hers.

"You're so fucking sexy." I manage between kisses. "This is something I've always wanted to do."

"What is?"

"Sex, in *public*," I say, unzipping her dress to the waist, exposing her to the steamy California heat.

Winnie moans as her body gets some air. She takes my hand and leads it under her dress. "Then shut up and *fuck* me."

My fingers rise up between her separated thighs as she hikes up her skirt, and before I can get ahold of her turns around, showing me her perfect ass. My eyes go wide when I see a sparkle between her cheeks. She looks at me with a grin.

"You naughty bunny, have you had that in all night?"

"Is that so bad?"

I lick my lips and press it like the little button that it is. She moans. "Not at all." I give it a few more taps and listen to her whimper before I finally uncage my aching cock. She leans forward, but I correct her. Pressing her against the cold brick building, I lift her leg and find the sweet spot. The plug makes for a tighter fit, so I go slower than I'd like. Winnie reaches back, grabbing my head as I kiss her neck.

"Would you fuck me already?" She demands, digging her nails into me. I start to go harder, and she pushes off the wall, grinding against me. Moans become yips, and yips become mutual yelps. I have to cover her mouth with my hand to silence her and bite down on her shoulder to quell my own voice as I come.

Leaning against her, I pant like I've just run a marathon, my cock still twitching deep in her. "I love you." I sigh.

"I love you too." She says with her head on my shoulder. "Let's go home."

By the time we get back around the front of Sweet'ums, the Uber has arrived, we climb inside, and she leans forward to give him the address to her house. I, of course, strategically place my hand, so she sits on it. She wiggles, and it's a bit like playing Tetris. Jackpot. I've got the plug and am gently and rhythmically pushing it as we go. She grasps my thigh tightly, trying hard to keep her composure. *Trying* being the core word here. Not caring if the driver gets a show, I lean over and fish for a kiss. Winnie lets out a ravenous moan, and our tongues battle for supremacy.

I hear the driver clear his throat but ignore him when she climbs into my lap. Our makeout session ends with her cum on me as we pull up the drive. Paying the driver, I toss her over my shoulder, and into the house we go.

***

Showered and with fresh sheets on the bed, I watch Winnie as she curls into me. This is the first time I've been in bed with a woman for more than a quick fuck in twenty-five years. It's strange. I'm not really sure what to do or how to be. I keep trying not to fidget.

"Are you okay?" Winnie asks, sitting up and flipping on the bedside light.

"Yeah, just-I'm trying to get comfortable. This is new to me." May as well be honest.

"It's been a while for me too but think of it as cuddling."

"Also, a new concept." I look away, somewhat embarrassed.

"What are you used to?" She's looking at me, confused.

Can't tell her that! "I haven't shared a bed since my divorce. I was only married eighteen months, and she was pregnant ten of those, So you can imagine how we slept. Gabby wasn't a really affectionate woman." I sit up and sigh. "Sex, sex was her thing, she was good at it, took control of me with it, that's for sure. There was never any of this." I point between us. "No sharing, or real intimacy. I like to *touch*, I like to *be* touched, just have never really had the types of relationships that went that way. So I'm not sure how all this is supposed to happen."

RESOLUTION

"How did you expect us to sleep when we move in?" Winnie watches me. "Would it make you feel better if I had something on?"

"No, it's not that. I think I've just got a bit of anxiety. I can't help but wonder what happens if I roll over in the night and crush you?"

"You're not going to crush me." She laughs. "Did Sofia never climb in bed with you as a child?"

I shake my head, "She'd come in the room but always to wake me up. I'd check and spray for monsters, then she'd go right back to sleep. I mean, she'd fallen asleep in the room before, but I again always put her to bed."

Winnie shakes her head. "We'll take this easy. What side do you like best?"

"I'm where I can be if I wanna try and hold you. These stitches are a bitch to sleep on."

"Okay, next thing then. Would you rather me face you or me face away?"

"Face me, I would think. If you face away, I'm liable to choke on your hair in the night." I smirk. "I would like to try and just get comfortable together."

"Do you want me to get the fire going or maybe the tv? Will that help?"

I run my hand down my face. "I feel like a toddler, you're trying to coax to bed. It's like you've read me the story, you've tucked me in, and now I gotta pee. I'm sorry." I chuckle, grabbing her. "Come here. I think I'm just overthinking it all."

"I want you to be comfortable, or you won't sleep, and we have to get the kids in less than twelve hours."

"Well, how do you think we should? I mean, what works for you? Maybe if you are more on me than next to me?"

"You want me on top of you? Are you trying to fuck us both unconscious?"

"You said whatever works." I snicker. "No, seriously, I mean it, if you're on me, then no limbs fall asleep, just the body, and I can hold you and not worry about smooshing you in the night."

"If your cock hits me, I'm going to want it, then you're going to get woke up no matter what. I'm just warning you now. Let's try this." She reaches over and shuts out the light. "How do you want me?"

"Loaded question." I kiss her softly. "I suppose just climb on and make yourself comfortable. Head on my chest, legs, however, you need. Worse case? You slide off and into a more comfortable position in the night."

"If you let me hit the floor, you're going to be in big trouble," Winnie says, straddling me and then laying her head on my chest. Her weight on me is calming, and the smell of her hair even more so. I rub my hand down her back, lazily the motion relaxing us both, and soon I feel my eyes growing heavy. Sleep is not far off.

RESOLUTION

Chapter 35-Winnie

Packing has begun. With less than a month till the kids and I move into Jarrett's, there are boxes all over my house. This coming weekend we start painting. Since the kids are helping, we just have to keep an eye on them. I'm back to work finally. Even taken care of Sofia a couple of times. She comes in at least twice a week to be pampered. Is it bad we've been arguing with the kids about what is going and what's staying? They want everything! It's a normal Wednesday night. I'm heading to pick up Rumor, Ivy, and Iris and make it to Crew's basketball game.

I park in front of the school because I have to get Allyson and Addyson out of their car seats. I've got Ally, and Echo has Addy. We go in to get the other three. I spot Rumor but not Ivy or Iris.

"Rumor? Where are the girls?"

"Um-" She looks around. "They were here. I had to pee." She points to the bleachers. "Mister McCormick was here, though."

Fuck! "Okay, take Ally and go sit down for me." I try not to panic as I make my way over to Linda. "Where are Ivy and Iris?"

"They left with Brad. He said he had talked to you."

"Well, he hadn't. You should have called me!" I practically shout as I run back to the other four. Picking both Ally and Addy up. "Echo, help Rumor to get her stuff, and let's go."

Getting everyone in the car, I grab my phone calling Jarrett.

"Hey, you guys on the way? I was thinking maybe we could go get pizza after the game."

"Is Ivy and Iris there?" I ask, panicked, but hoping Brad took them to Crew's game.

Silence for a moment. "Winnie, what's going on? Why would they be here? How could they be here?"

"Brad picked them up. Tell Piper to meet me outside to take these four." I jump into the car and drive fifty or so feet to the middle school.

"O-Okay. I'm coming." He says, and I can hear him talking, and the voices start mingling together. Within moments here comes the Calvary. Piper, Brent with his daughter Clara, Bryce, and Tatum. I'm guessing Austin is holding seats with his crutches and all. At the front is Jarrett.

"We're here." He says, wrapping his arm around me.

RESOLUTION

"I'll take the little ones," Bryce says quickly, going for the back seat as Piper and Tatum come up to me.

"Linda, let him take them. Apparently, he said he talked to me. I didn't even know he was in town." I run a shaking hand over my face.

"Have you tried calling them?"

"No, my name will come up. He won't let them answer. Clara! Can you call Iris? Ivy will ignore it. She's still mad."

With a nod, Clara pulls her cell phone from her shirt. Guess boob carrying is back in style. She scrolls and dials. A few seconds later, she just looks at me. "I'm sorry, aunt Win, it went straight to voicemail." She tilts the phone toward me.

"I'm calling the cops." Jarrett hisses, "He could have them halfway out of town by now."

"Why did they go with him?" I'm crying. "I need to get my papers out of my purse. The police are going to need them."

"Auntie Win, I'm sorry. I shouldn'ta left the court like I did." Rumor sniffles.

"This isn't your fault, Rumor. Why don't you and Echo go cheer on Crew, huh? There's signs in the back that Ally, Addy, and your sister made."

"Wh-wh-what about Iris and Ivy? Are they gonna be okay?" She's on the verge of a full-on ugly cry.

"They'll be just fine. I promise." I need to calm myself while the kids are around.

Tatum grabs the posters from the back. "Come on, girls, let's go make Crew's cheering squad really loud. You too, Clara."

The nudge is enough to get the girls moving, as Bryce has already carried the little ones off, leaving me with Piper, Brent, and Jarrett, who is off on the phone.

"I just don't understand. They both know better. I get Ivy going, but not Iris. Where do you think he's taking them?"

"When it comes to that asshole, it's hard to say. I just can't believe he's stupid enough to pull this in the first place." Brent says with a shake of his head.

"Does he know you're moving in with Jarrett?" Piper asks.

"Not that I know of." I turn, looking at Jarrett. "Are they on their way?"

He comes walking over to me. "They are sending a squad over now."

"Has any of them said anything to you about talking to Brad?" I ask him.

"No, they don't talk about him. I mean, Iris is all about the new house wanting to know what it has, and Ivy, she hardly speaks to me, you know that." Jarrett says frustratingly. "I should have been paying more attention. Should have seen something like this coming."

"This isn't your fault any more than it is mine," I say, wrapping my arms around his waist and laying my head on his chest. "I'm so scared. What if he's gone?"

"Chiquita?" I feel Brenton's hand on my back. "Don't you have that GPS tracker on their phones, like I have on Clara?"

"I completely forgot," I say, fumbling with my phone. I'm shaking so bad I almost drop it.

RESOLUTION

Piper takes my phone. "I've got it."

The white Jetta pulls up. Isaiah behind the wheel, Jeremiah and Dante hopping out the right passenger side.

"Hey, have you found them yet?" Isaiah calls.

"What happened?" Comes from Jeremiah."

Jarrett looks at me. He hasn't met Piper's boys yet. Or at least he hasn't realized that he has. Isaiah hangs around at Sweet'ums while Jeremiah works with his mom at her shop. The thing is, they take after their daddy, with smooth ebony skin and wide smiles full of mischief.

"Jeremiah and Isaiah are Piper's boys and the oldest in the group," I say, trying to clue him in.

"You must be Jarrett. Wish we could have met on better circumstances." Jeremiah says.

Jarrett looks at him and his brother. I can't describe the look, but if I were to try, I'd say it's a mixture of confusion and humor mixed with anxiety. In other words, he was having a small conniption. Before he can say anything, the whoop-whoop of a police car can be heard, and my attention is broken, turned toward the squad car and its approach.

It takes damn near an hour to get the report filed, but then I'm told they can't submit for twenty-four hours. Which has caused me to completely flip my shit! Can't submit them for twenty-four hours. I've heard a lot of bull shit.

"That was fucking pointless," I say as the cops are getting in the car. "Piper, did you find them?"

"They're at the airport," Piper says, looking from Jarrett and me to Brent.

"Where the fuck could he be taking them?"

"He can't take them out of the country without a passport," Piper says.

"Can someone take Crew with them? I've got to go. Jarrett, maybe you should stay with him."

"Out of the question. If he puts up any sort of fight, you'll need to be able to get the girls and get out of there. I'll drive. You call the airport and speak to the Transit Authority." Jarrett insists.

"My car or yours?" I ask, pulling my keys out.

"Take mine." Piper tosses her keys to Jarrett. Mustang it is.

I toss her mine as Jarrett tosses his to Brent. "Let's go," I say and take off running for the mustang. Jarrett right on my ass.

Chapter 36-Jarrett

Winnie is a mess of emotions. Fear, anger, anxiety. She managed to get ahold of the security office at San Jose International. She explained the situation, and they have agreed to look into it. In the meantime, we are making the forty-five-minute drive out there. She hasn't stopped shaking that leg. She's chewing on the side of her thumb.

"Reach into my leg pocket," I say as I make the loop from Colman Ave to Airport Boulevard.

"What could you possibly need at this moment?" She snaps.

"Not me. *You*." I manage to get the wheel set and dig my hand into my pants cargo pocket to reveal an unopened pack of Salems. I grab the cigarettes and lighter, handing them to her. "Here."

She looks down at my hand then back to me before finally taking the pack. She shakes so badly as she lights the cigarette. Inhales, and then she hands it to me. Okay so, we're cheating.

"Can we go any faster?"

"Only if you want to get pulled over and arrested. Security here is no fucking joke when it comes to trivial bullshit. It's just another mile. I take a drag, the smoke fills my lungs, and I sigh, passing it back to her. "We're gonna get them back." I try and assure her.

"We can claim insanity. I'm menopausal."

I chuckle, "Only if you were driving." I pull up to the drop off and let her out. "I'm going to park, see if you can get any member of the TSA to help you. But Winnie, be calm about it. They won't help you if you get hysterical."

She flicks the cigarette and is out of the car with a nod. By the time I get to the entrance, I can already hear her. She's pushing her paperwork into the hands of a guard as three more have their hands up, trying to calm her down.

"Ma'am, we can't help you if you don't slow down. We can't just let you through the security checkpoint without identification and a scan."

"Here." I interrupt. "Honey, you forgot your pocketbook. "I'm Jarrett Brooks, this is Winnie McCormick, she is these little girls mom. Their father is currently here in the airport, attempting to leave with them."

"We have been alerted of the situation." A woman TSA agent explains. "We can look up his name. If his flight hasn't left, we can delay it and retrieve the children in question."

"Can't you just let me in to find them? *Please*," Winnie begs.

"I'm sorry, ma'am, we have protocols. We can't-"

"Missus McCormick?" A man's authoritative voice breaks through the annoying woman's speech. Winnie's head spins in his direction. "I'm Officer Richmond. We spoke on the phone. We have located your ex-husband's ticket. He has booked a one-way flight to Seattle for himself and two minors. We have delayed the flight, and agents are currently looking for them. If you would accompany me, we will get your girls." He points to a golf cart looking thing. "It's a long way to the United terminal. This will be faster."

She grabs my hand and pulls me along. "Let's get ou-the girls."

Our? I can't help but smile slightly as we get on the cart. The agent takes off, zipping through the checkpoints. We have to go outside to cross the tarmac before reaching the boarding area. Upon arrival, Winnie's eyes dart around, and the agent goes to an attendant. I see heads shake, and confused looks take hold. I grasp her hand.

"They have to be here." She sobs as the agent approaches.

"They haven't called their section yet. So he isn't on the plane. Security checks say they have come through. They just haven't arrived here yet.

They have to be-," Winnie takes off, and I'm hot on her heels.

I know what she's thinking. We had to have passed them in this sea of people. She's backtracking as her bag starts ringing. She'd passed it to me, and I still have it. Fishing as I run, trying to catch her, she runs exceptionally fast for a woman with short legs.

"Hello?" I say out of breath.

Sniff. "Jar-rett? Where's mom?" Iris's voice comes through the line.

I stop cold. "Winnie!" I scream. "Iris? Are you okay? Where are you? Are you in the airport?" I can hear banging and what I'm pretty sure is Ivy's voice in the background.

"Iris hang up now! We're getting away. Dad wants us."

"I don't want to go with Dad!" Sniff. "I'm in the bathroom. Ivy is screaming at me."

Winnie turns back, looking at me. "What's going on? Why did you stop?"

"It's Iris." I let her see the phone. "She's locked herself in a bathroom stall. I don't- Iris, hon, listen, your mom and I are here. But there are a lot of bathrooms, did you see anything nearby? A shop or restaurant so your mom can get to you?"

"Um, Jamba Juice. I remember seeing that before coming in here."

"Iris open this door. Daddy is going to come in here." Ivy is screaming. My eyes dart around. I point down the long walk.

"Winnie, the Jamba Juice, they're in the bathroom." It's as I say it that I see Brad lingering, then his head picks up. He must hear Ivy screaming. I grab Winnie, and we run for it. Brad has gone into the bathroom. Winnie is ahead of me, and she runs straight for him. He smacks her, and she hits the floor. I'm on him in an instant. I hear Ivy screaming as I get him in a headlock. I feel my stitches rip, but I don't care. This son of a bitch is not laying another hand on these girls. Any of them. I hear him choking as the Agents come rushing in.

"Mister Brooks, please let him go!" I'm ordered as I continue to squeeze. I don't let go until I feel him go limp, and then I drop him to the ground like the sack of shit he is. The agents descend on him as I go to Winnie. Ivy is in the corner, knees to her chest as she sobs. Iris comes rushing out and straight to her mom.

"Are you okay?" Winnie is looking her over before looking around. Her eyes land on Ivy. "Hold her." She passes Iris to me, and Iris just clings to me. Winnie tries to hold Ivy and gets shoved away. "Please don't-just let me hold you."

"I hate you. I hate him. I want to go with Dad!"

"You can't."

"Dad's going to court, and he's taking us away from you! You don't love us. All you worry about is Jarrett! I can tell them who I want to live with."

"Ivy, please don't do this. I love you. I love you more than I love myself. Please just come home with us."

"Then why do we have to live with him? Why does he have to be in our life?" Ivy is screaming again, and everyone is watching.

Winnie looks at me with tears falling as they cart Brad away.

"Ivy-" I start. "You don't have to like me, I wish you would, but you need to understand that what you are doing is wildly unfair to your mom. It's okay with you that your dad has a new wife, a new baby, but your mom can't have me. For shame. I'm sorry you feel this way, but I love your mom, and I'm not going anywhere."

Chapter 37 Winnie

The ride from the airport to my place is silent. Nobody speaks, and if I weren't sure we were all alive, I'd think no one was even breathing. Pulling up to my house, it's packed. When I say packed, I mean filled to the brim. Austin and his three, Piper with the boys, Brenton and Clara, Bryce, and his three are here. Pretty sure I spotted Tatum's car as well.

I sigh, getting out of Piper's car. The girls are out and running for the house. Me? I'm falling into Jarrett's arms.

"I don't know what to do. I don't want her to hate either of us."

"You're her mother. She loves you. She's just angry. She needs time." I hear him hesitate, making me look up. "Maybe someone to talk to?"

"Maybe, I just-I don't know. Are we moving too fast?" Even asking the question has me shaking my head. "I love you, but-"

I'm cut off by Crew screaming. "Ivy and Iris are fighting."

"Fuck." I don't even think as I pull Jarrett along. As we get through the door, I see Brenton holding Ivy and Bryce with Iris. "What in the hell is going on here?"

"Iris slugged Ivy!" Brenton grits out as my quiet little girl growls like a Hellcat.

"She deserved it! Jarrett actually loves us! Daddy cares more about what it looks like! I like how it looks! I want a real daddy!" She collapses in Brenton's arms, sobbing.

I'm standing with my eyes bouncing back and forth, watching the kids. I'm not even sure what to say. My entire family is here watching this all go down.

"Daddy loves us. He said so! Mom and Jarrett only love each other. We are gonna move in, and then they're gonna have another baby. They'll forget about us." Ivy spits.

My breath catches in my chest as I drop to my knees in front of them. "I don't know what to do anymore. I think you three are happy, and I finally decided to let myself find what I've been missing. Why is that so bad? Do you want me single forever?" I look between Ivy and Iris.

"I want you with Daddy." Ivy cries.

"Dad hates her. She deserves to be with someone that loves her. Jarrett wants us to be with him."

RESOLUTION

"Ivy," Bryce says, still holding on to her. "Not all mommies and daddies are meant to be together. We've talked about this." He crouches down, making her look at me. "Look at your mom. Look what your selfishness is doing to her. Until recently, when was the last time you remember her smiling?"

"Bryce don't do that," Jarrett says with a soft, almost defeated tone. "Don't dismiss how she feels. Look, know you think I want to take your mom away, but that's not the case. I don't just want her. I want all of you, including that weirdo dog. I want your daddy to be able to come and see you. I would never stop that, but he has made that difficult with his actions. I know-" He squats down- "That you don't trust me, I respect that. But maybe trust that your mom loves you at least as much as your dad, trust that she has put you first all your life, and always will. Just because she loves me doesn't mean she loves you any less. In fact, it means she loves you more. She loves you enough to want to share how wonderful you are with someone else. That is the sacrifice of love." He looks at me and then Ivy again. "Please let me love you too."

I can't keep the tears back anymore as I wait for Ivy to say something. My tears have apparently broken two of my children. Iris and Crew have wrapped their arms around me.

"I'm sorry for fighting," Iris says.

"I'm sorry Ivy is bullheaded and doesn't listen." Crew lets go and looks at his sister. "If anyone has the right to be upset over Jarrett, it should be me. I was the man of the house, and he's stepping all over my territory." He looks at Jarrett. "I want to thank you for helping our mom and us. If it weren't for you, we'd still be listening to her cry every night. Sometimes it's over the most stupid things, but Brenton says Menopause causes that. He also says if you throw chocolate at them, they won't try to eat you. Ivy may not want you around yet, but Iris and I voted. Two against one-wins. We love how you love us and want you to stay around. We want to move in with you because if we do, our mom doesn't cry over the bills anymore or keeping food on the table."

I drop my head and just let my tears fall because if my twelve year old sees all of that, I'm not doing my job. I swallow hard, "Ivy, please don't make me choose. Please don't make your siblings choose."

"I want to live with dad," Ivy says, almost as if she could care less how we all feel.

"Fine, I'll think about it tonight and let you know my answer tomorrow. Just go take your shower." The words fly out of my mouth before I even know what I'm saying. "I love you, Ivy. I always will."

Her response is to stomp up the stairs, and all I can do is sit here and hold the other two.

"Winnie?" I hear Tatum and can feel the others around me. "It's been a long night. Do you want us to stay?"

Before I can answer, I feel my babies letting me go, and I'm lifted into strong arms. "If you want to help, they need to eat, I'm guessin' you all do, so while I get this settled, why don't you

RESOLUTION

figure out supper." Jarrett cradles me into him. "Come on, my girl. Let's get you cleaned up."

I don't speak until we're behind closed doors. "She hates me. Hates me enough to leave. Maybe I should let her go. Let her see the grass isn't always greener."

He sets me down, "Tatum is right. It's been a long and emotional night. Let's just wait. Things may look different in the morning. She watched me choke her dad out. I'm sure that hasn't helped the situation." He sighs. "I will not let you lose her, and I will not be driven away by her either. At the end of the day, she is the child, and you are the parent. Now, go take a shower and come down to those other people that love you." He kisses me softly. "I'll be here."

I pull him along with me. "I'm not ready for you to let me go yet. So, I guess we're taking one together."

Chapter 38 Jarrett

I rub my face. Seems I crashed along with the puppy pile. After I consoled Winnie in the way she needed, we came downstairs to find Piper and Brenton pulling together stuff to go outside while their kids entertained Iris and Crew. They ordered pizza for the lot and suggested we watch a movie on Disney Plus. Turns out Winnie's huge back yard set up is completed by a roll-out movie screen.

Blankets and pillows line the raised tongue and groove patio floor as I see the sleeping kids, including Ivy, who apparently got lonely.

I wiggle out from under Winnie and Piper. That's all I needed was to have my girl see her BFF snuggled up on me. With light steps, I head for the bathroom. The day's activities have my arm screaming. I tore more than a dozen stitches, but we just butterflied them shut because I

RESOLUTION

refused to go back to the hospital. I trudge upstairs to find some Tylenol. Tossing back a handful, I am set to return to the squishy couches when I walk into the kitchen.

"Sofia?" I was confused, as she wasn't here earlier. She's leaning against the kitchen island with a piece of pizza and Brenton Sweet.

She puts down the food and comes around to me, hugging me. "Daddy, I came as soon as I got your message."

"That was six hours ago," I say softly. "You should have gone home." I look over her shoulder at Brenton, who's practically making a point of *not* looking at me. "Is uh- something going on?"

"Daddy, no. I was just hungry and saw the food. Brenton was keeping me company. I also asked him if I could come to work after I have Scotty."

"Uh-huh, so why didn't I see you on my way through?" I can't help the pit in my stomach.

"Jarrett, I saw the car pull up while I was having a smoke, so I let her in. Ain't nothing sordid going on."

"Sorry, it's just been that kind of day." I chuckle as Sofia leans on me.

"You're a fuddy-duddy, daddy." She smiles. "Is everybody okay?"

"Physically, though I think emotionally, we're all fucked."

"I'm sorry." She stretches. "Where can a pregnant woman put her feet up?"

"There's a recliner in the living room." Brenton points behind us.

"I'm sleepy, daddy. I've got a full belly, so I'm gonna crash." She kisses my cheek, and taking the last bite of her slice, leaves me with Brenton.

"She's a good kid." He says, putting her plate in the dishwasher.

"Yeah, *my* good kid."

Brenton's shoulders shake with a laugh. "Jarrett, I'm not looking for anything strange or familiar. Clara is more than enough for me to handle. I'm sure you understand."

"Look, I know my kid. Just- she can be persuasive is all. I'm trying to warn you."

He nods. "Well, thank you, and let me return the favor. Don't move forward if you don't plan to make it forever. If you are test running Winnie, let it be. Those kids don't deserve to have to try and survive her losing another man she gave her heart to."

"I-"

He cuts me off. "Look, I've been around since before, Bradly. I'll be around long after if you fuck up. I'm just telling you now that if I have to pick her up off the floor because of you, the next time one of your houses collapses, you will be in it."

"I hear you."

"Do you, though? I mean, I could write volumes on what you don't know about Winnie, about Bradly, or these kids. Do you know why she doesn't talk to her mother or father? Why she's never gone back to Nevada? You may want to have a conversation or two, is all I'm saying. Better learn it now then after you make them all love you." He pats my shoulder, making me wince as he heads back downstairs to go outside one more.

I sit on the front stairs smoking one from my stash, watching the sun peek out over the city when I feel a hand touch my shoulder. Looking up, I see Winnie wrapped up like a burrito in a throw. With a short smile, she takes the cigarette and sits next to me.

She takes a long smooth drag, then hands it back. "What's the matter?"

I sigh. "Everything, nothing. I just couldn't sleep. Too much happening, I suppose." I put my good arm around her. "We can't let Ivy leave."

"I don't think we can make her stay." She answers sadly.

"She may not have a choice." I pass her my phone. "When was the last time you looked at the news?" I press play. It's a report about a quarantined ship carrying people with a communicable disease off our coast. "They say there's been a case just north of us."

Winnie's eyes fly to mine. "I haven't really had time. It's been so crazy the last two months. She won't have much choice. I just don't know what kind of fight it will be."

"If this thing is contagious like they say, we tell her it's dangerous for her little brother, that her flying could make him sick. I mean, it sounds like airports are a brewing ground for this shit."

"Yeah, she'll just have to hate us." Winnie shrugs, taking another drag from the cigarette.

"I love you, and we are going to make this work. She's afraid of us not loving her, so let's show her how much her happiness means to us.

Don't go to the police station this morning. I know it goes against everything I feel, too, but maybe if we show mercy, show we are not like other parents who don't care about their own, then maybe she can start to trust." I don't want to bring up the things Brenton mentioned. Still, perhaps in a roundabout way, I can get my answers organically through conversation.

Chapter 39 Winnie

Parent's that don't care about their own. That statement makes me chuckle, which has Jarrett watching me. I haven't told him about my parents. The only ones that know everything is our core group. Considering they were all there when I was almost thrown into jail for gambling, they should. I sigh- might as well spill my guts.

"Wanna take a bath with me?" I ask Jarrett.

"You wanna take a bath? *Now?*" He asks, confused. "We got a backyard full of kids."

"And three adults here to help if need be, but the teens will keep ou-the children company. We need to talk and somewhere more private with a bottle of Maker's Mark. Maybe you won't need it, but I will."

He flicks the butt to the street. "Seeing as I haven't slept, I guess you can't call it day drinking." He stands and puts out his hand to me. "Come on, my girl."

"You go start the bath, and I'll grab the bottle."

I spotted Brenton as I was pulling the bottle from the cabinet. No words needed to be spoken. He knows if I need this, whatever is going on is either a good thing, or I'm about to have a conversation I don't want to be having. I drag myself up the stairs. Maybe I'm a little slower than need be, but it gives me time to gather my nerves. Locking the door and flipping on the music *Rescue Me* by OneRepublic fills the room.

Jarrett is already sunken down into the bubbly water. I hand him the bottle so I can strip my clothes. I don't speak until I'm settling my body against his, but I can feel his eyes on me the entire time. I take the bottle from him to open and take a big swig. Liquid courage never hurt.

"I'm guessin' we're in for a soul-bearing experience?" His fingers gently run up my arm. "You don't have to explain anything. I don't care who you were."

"The story I'm about to tell you could change our entire relationship, but it's something you should know before we go any further."

"Unless you're about to tell me that you were born a boy and that Bradly was really their mom, I doubt that very much." He smiles against my back as he leaves a small trail of kisses.

"I was born with all the same parts I have today, but I wasn't born in the United States. My

RESOLUTION

birthplace is in Madrid, Spain. When I was two, my parents moved me to Las Vegas, Nevada, because that is where my father's family was." I stop taking another big swig and sigh heavily. "Piper and I both grew up on the streets of Vegas. Everyone talks about it being a cool place to visit. It's not. Vegas is a place where you grow up before your time. To be honest, Piper and I hated one another for a long, long time. Different crowds and all. I'm sure you know what Vegas is good for, even if you've never been." I pause, giving him time to speak if he wants.

"You said you came out here for college. Was that not the only reason?"

"I came to get away from my parents. You said that thing about parents that care about their children, and it brought a lot up. My parents gambled a lot. It's a trade they instilled into well-*me*. By the time I was five, I was counting cards. By twelve, I was being used in private games. I ran away. I never planned to go back. Then there was this one day after my twenty-first birthday, we were partying. When I say we, I mean only four of us, as the other two were still in high school. Piper was twenty, but well, we both had a fake ID long before we should have. Austin is a year older than me. Benton, as you know, is the oldest of us. He was twenty-seven at the time." I need more liquid courage. Jarrett is being so quiet, and at this moment, that scares me more.

He sighs against me as he wraps his arms around me. "Something tells me I'll never vay-cay in Vegas with you. Which is fine as I hate the desert."

"No, no, you won't." One more drink, and then it's back to storytelling. "My father showed up at the door. My parents were in so much debt that a not so good person was holding my mother. He asked for money, but I didn't have on me how much he needed. He knew I could make what he needed in a weekend, and I could. I didn't want to, but I also couldn't let her die. This wasn't the first time he came and got me for help. Piper and I looked at each other. She knew what was coming. Tickets booked. We caught a flight out that night. Once we landed and got all dolled up, the tables were just starting groves. Piper, Brenton, and Austin mostly played the slots. While I was at the blackjack table. Do you have any idea how long some of the people sit there for?" I shake my head. "I went in with ten grand. I needed to more than triple it." I can't stop the tears from falling. With a sniff, I continue yet again. "I was five hundred short from having what I needed when I was picked up and carted out. The owner of the casino I was in changed hands. The new owner knew me from when I was younger. I almost went to jail that night, but it's also the night I vowed to never set foot back in Vegas. I can't go into any casino because of the stunt I pulled. My parents ended up getting the money, but it wasn't because of me."

"You were put in a terrible and unfair position. I'm sorry that happened to you. It wasn't your fault." He hugs me a little tighter, wincing as I'm sure his stitches are being pulled.

"I guess I was very lucky. My parents were good to me. I lost my dad when I was twenty-four to lung cancer and my mom... A year later of a broken heart. It's why Sofia is adamant I quit, both smoking and Gabby. Neither were ever very good for me."

I lean over the side of the tub so I can put the bottle on the floor before turning my body so I can staddle Jarrett. I want to see his face.

"I think I dealt with Bradley for so long because, in a way, he reminds me of my parents. He loves control, and I let him have it. It wasn't until we split up that I finally got a backbone. I just thought you should know my crazy before we move further."

"Winnie, none of that is who you are now. It's not what I see. I see a woman that has surpassed obstacles and found herself. A woman not afraid to admit she is afraid is the strongest woman in the world, and I'm honored to be in this tub and this life with you." He shifts, and I can feel his cock rise beneath me. "Now, I think that you need to work off that booze." He smiles, and just as he thrusts, a knock comes on the door.

"Mommy! I need to pee, and everyone else is in a toilet!" Little Iris's voice comes barreling through the door. "I'm going to hell," I mumble as Jarrett just laughs.

Chapter 40 Jarrett

Cock blocked by a nine-year-old. I give a good thrust, and Winnie is pushing me under the water as she gets out.

"I'm coming, baby." She wraps a towel around herself. "Stay down."

I get as low as I can, but it's not going to matter. She has to pass me to get to the little room with the toilet.

The door opens, and Iris zips by. She's got her shorts half down before she even gets there. I hear the little sigh of relief and try not to laugh. Winnie steps in front of the tub. I assume she's trying to block me. There's a flush.

"Mommy, what are you doing?" Iris asks.

"Nothing, just standing here. I was in the tub when you knocked."

"With Jarrett?"

"Um-"

RESOLUTION

"I needed help because of my stitches," I say, my head popping over the top. I'm glad the bubbles haven't totally evaporated yet.

Iris doesn't look convinced. "Umm-" She runs out of the room, and all I hear is her screaming. "Mommy and Jarrett are making babies!"

I facepalm, my rager falling flat. I shake my head. "Well, now that the whole house knows where we are."

Winnie drops her towel and climbs back in the tub. "No sense in going out there yet. Too many people in the kitchen for that." She grabs my cock and starts stroking. I stay her hands. "I'd much rather be fucking you in that bed. I don't wanna drown trying to eat that delicious pussy of yours."

She hops out of the tub, "You gotta catch me, first.." Soaked, she stands watching me. Up I come, and she gives chase, running for the carpeted walk-in closet. I grab her about the middle, and she squeals as I kiss and bite her shoulder.

"You're mine now," I say heavily as she spins and pulls me down to the floor.

"Is that so?" She smirks, wrapping her legs around me. "I may be on the bottom, but I'm still the top in this relationship." Grabbing my cock again, she leads me to where she wants me, and I'm happy to satisfy her needs. I grind down into her, and she lets out a ravenous moan. We may have a challenging day ahead, but if we can try and start those days like this, I think we may just make it.

***

Carnal desires satiated, we come downstairs and find that it's just the kids-my Sofia and her three. Sofia is plating breakfast, it would seem. I get a quirked brow with a little smile.

I look at Winnie and shrug.

"Don't you shrug, daddy. If you all are fixing to make us siblings, we should know about it." She sets a hand to her hip. "There's a lot of prep for a baby, and we are headed for some rocky roads if the news is right."

"First, not that it's any of your fours business. I'm on birth control, and I'm going through menopause. If a baby makes it through that, it damn sure belongs here, but the statics are not high that I will get pregnant."

"Mmhmm." Comes from my daughter. "So you have seen the crazy about that Chinese stuff? They're saying people need to like stay six feet apart and wash their hands while singing happy birthday. Craziness, right?"

"Mommy?" Iris says with concern in her voice. "What's social distancing?"

Winnie is making her coffee as she answers. "Well, it means we'll have to stand so far apart from other people. Like you won't be able to hug those that aren't in your home. Or, like when we're in the store, you wouldn't just touch everything like you all do. Does that make sense?"

"So Ivy won't be able to hug her boyfriend then? Good, that means we won't get Momo like Crew." Iris says thoughtfully.

"Hey, I take offense to that." Crew pipes up.

"Shut up, Crew. It's Mono, not Momo, and you get that from kissing. If I have to worry about that with the two of you, then all three of you are grounded for the foreseeable future."

"Mom!" Ivy stomps her foot. "If I stay, I want to see Kris! He's nice to me and to look at, and he's eleven!"

"Sure, you've got a smartphone. Go call him on video."

I run my hand through my hair. "Sofia on steroids," I mumble. "Chastity belts! I need chastity belts! Stat!"

"If you're making babies, I'm putting my order in for boys." Crew says with a mouthful of eggs.

"So glad this one is a Scotty and not a Mary." Sofia rubs her ever-growing belly. "Crew, you can hope, but he got me, so it looks like girls are in your future."

"Enough, no babies. We got enough with you four." I say. "Now, can we eat, or do I have to have cold eggs like the first eighteen years of that one's life?" I point at my daughter.

Crew drops his head to the table. "I need manly activities. Something without all these girls. Couldn't you have had a boy? No offense Sofia your pretty and all but balls over boobs *any* day."

"How's about this, Crew? Would you like to learn to safely use some power tools? Maybe do some framing and sheetrock installation? I thought since there are so many of you kids, and we have the property at the new house, we could build you all a clubhouse out back." I smile as he picks up his head.

"Yes! Mom, I'm going to stay with Jarrett."

"Hey, what about me?" Iris pouts, crossing her arms.

"Balls over boobs, Iris." Crew tells his sister.

I look at Winnie. "I'm not in this. You started it."

"I was thinking more like over summer break. And Iris, if you want to help, you can help me design it. How's that sound?"

"Sexist!" Sofia chirps. "Get her some pink power tools and show her too."

I shake my head. "I am the last person you should call sexist. Didn't I encourage your football and dancing? I'm an equal opportunity, daddy!"

"I want to work with tools! Mommy, tell him I listen better."

"My name is Bennett, and I'm not in it."

I look at Winnie. "What?" I shake my head. "Okay, never heard that."

"As in, leave me out of it?" She shakes her head. "How do you put up with him?"

Sofia shrugs. "You get used to it. I mean, he really is just a big ole teddy bear. Give him a hug, and he's putty in your hands." My little girl comes over to me and hugs me. I smile. "And besides, it makes snatching his credit cards easier!" She snickers running away with my wallet!

"Sofia!" I scold, "Give it back."

"But daddy? Money!" She blows me a kiss, and I go back to eating my now cold eggs.

RESOLUTION

Chapter 41 Winnie

Schools are closed, and I am done! If I was thinking about more kids, that would be flying out the window about now. With eleven kids under one roof, I'm losing my fucking mind. Isaiah and Jeremiah, the two seventeen-year-olds, are helping Crew, Ivy, and Iris. While Dante and Clara, who both have turned sixteen this month, have split up. Clara took Rumor and Echo, the seven-year-olds helping them pack the basement. Dante is by far the best child in my house at this moment. He's got the three-year-olds Addyson and Allyson keeping them occupied. Last I checked, they were outside.

I hit the talk button on my ringing phone but scream upstairs instead of answering. "Ivy, Iris split up. Crew and Isaiah, just pack and shut the hell up!" I sigh before putting the phone to my ear, "Hello?"

RESOLUTION

"You about ready to run away?" I can hear the laughter in Jarrett's voice.

"I'd go back to Vegas to get away from this. You're taking some of them with you when you leave."

"How about this, I've got a few buckets of fried chicken with all the trimmings when I've sufficiently stuffed them, and they get all sleepy I'll stuff you then take all the boys and your girls back to my place to work. This way, you can take a nap with the little ones. Sound like a plan?"

"I was thinking something like that. The house is mostly done, is it not?"

"Just a few superficial things left. Mostly cosmetic. I was thinking if they're gonna be home, we could start the clubhouse and moving you in. I'm tired of sleeping alone."

"How far away are you?" I ask, as the screaming starts again. "We're going to be two fewer kids in about two seconds."

"I'm here." I can hear the truck pull up and head for the door, he's got all kinds of bags in his hands, and the truck is overflowing with materials. Thankfully, he got his stitches out before all this shit happened, as they are saying no hospital visits unless it's dire.

I drop my phone on the table and go out the door to help. "Let me help." I kiss him, hello.

"Sure." He passes me the mashed potatoes and wedges, keeping the chicken and coleslaw to himself.

"So, Austin and I spoke last night. He wants them to come home, but we both agreed that they may be safer with us." I look over my shoulder, hoping Jarrett takes it better than Crew.

"Wait, so you're saying that we're taking on two more kids, full time? Strike that- not kids- *girls*? Add to that Lulu, and I'm going to have to buy a freaking St. Bernard and call him Butch to balance the amount of estrogen running rampant." He chuckles. "Crew, get the door!"

"They're three, I was just thinking. I knew we made one of the rooms upstairs with us for Crew, but maybe we could put him in the basement and put Addy and Ally in there?"

"I just finished painting in there. He sighs. "Send me what you need for the room. I'll pick it up on the way home." He sounds thrilled, but willing.

"Hey, Jarrett," Dante's walking in, holding Ally and Addy's hands. "So, have you broken the news that you're stuck with us all for the next three weeks?"

"Dante, go get everyone washed up for lunch!" I snap while pulling plates out—anything I can do to not look at Jarrett at this moment.

"Wait, what?" I feel hands grasp my arms. "Eleven kids? For three weeks? Don't they have, I don't know, parents? Why can't Tatum take a few?" He huffs. "You come live with me, and she can keep them all here. It'll be good practice for her. Hell, I'll give her Sofia!"

"Daddy!" Sofia chirps from behind us. "I heard that!"

"Good! More babies." He's muttering to himself.

RESOLUTION

"Remember, you love me." I give him the puppy dog look that works for the girls. "You knew when getting into this, I came with a big family."

"Oh, don't give me those big doe eyes. They are not a get out of jail free card. You will *so* be working off all my stress. You better bring home a ton of sandalwood oil."

"About that, Tatum is taking over the salon, and I'll be doing paperwork from home, but I can have stuff dropped off." I smile at him.

"Luck so being pushed. That's it. If you are strong enough to lift a screwdriver, you will be working for all of this insanity! No arguments. If it needs mudding, you will mud if it needs screwing- I'll do that forget it." He shakes his head and grabs me. "Now, either kiss me, or I'm bound to have a stroke."

I bring my mouth to his ear. "I think while everyone is eating, toys may be calling our names." I squeal as I'm hoisted up and over his shoulder.

"Dante be sure everyone eats. I've decided to take my meal in private." Grabbing my ass, he heads for the stairs.

He doesn't stop until he's throwing me on the bed. "Did you lock the door?" I ask with his mouth on mine as we're pulling at each other's clothes.

"Damnit." He growls, damn near falling off the bed. "I'll be so glad when we're in my King." He huffs, looking at the door. He stops, breathes, and then drops his pants and kicks off his sneakers. "You want a double or a triple play?"

"Question is, what are you wanting to feel today? Do you want extra vibrations, or are you planning to use your hands and thrust at the same time?" I lick my lips, watching him.

"I'm thinking that new double penetrator, you know the one I can wear, that vibrates. I love knowing the idea of getting to have you totally filled up." He stalks toward me with pure lust in his eyes.

I bite my lip, pulling the new toy from the chest. "This one?" I ask mischievously. Holding up the silicone anal strap complete with thrusters.

He pulls off his boxers and attacks. This is going to be an eventful afternoon.

RESOLUTION

Chapter 42 Jarrett

Shelter-In-Place. The day before St. Patrick's day, our entire county went on lockdown. Schools have closed, bars and other non-essential businesses have been urged to do the same. This means that Winnie's Salon and Spa is now shuttered and locked up. Brenton and Piper are still running their shops, only now it's all pick-up and delivery. Brenton is trying to get it done, but drivers are hard to come by. No one wants to be out in this crazy. Words like epidemic and pandemic are being tossed around, and there are rumors that this will only worsen.

Packing was put into overdrive. I told Winnie to stop organizing it and just get it in something we can carry. With eleven kids and a pregnant daughter, it's gotten done, but not without some strain. Everyone is sharing space. The basement which Sofia was taking on has now been broken up and sectioned off to make more rooms. I'm glad Dante, Isaiah, and Jeremiah are strong boys because I'd never have gotten the sheetrock moved alone. The three guys I had working for me are now collecting unemployment.

I'm coming out of the basement when I see Sofia leaned against the kitchen counter, working on a corn dog.

"Having fun?" I smile, wiping paint and dust off my hands.

"Daddy, explain to me why you're doing all this work? I mean, didn't you have guys to help?"

"Yes, but this isn't an essential thing. Neither is my business as it doesn't serve the public. So they get to collect while I put all of you to work."

"I'm not doing anything." She pouts. "Daddy, I'm bored."

"It's only been five days." I chuckle.

"Six! And a half!" She retorts. "You missed Tuesday, apparently."

My head shakes until I spy Winnie. She's in these little cotton yoga shorts and a spaghetti strap tank. She pads over to the stand-up freezer and rips it open, lifting her top so we can all see her polka dot sports bra.

"Hot flash?" I snicker.

"I swear it's a billion degrees in this house." Winnie looks at me, and I can see that her face is flushed.

Looking at my phone, I see it's barely seventy degrees. In other words, it's fucking beautiful outside. "I can have the boys open a few more windows. Or if you really can't deal with it, go up

RESOLUTION

to our room, shut the door, and crank the AC. All the rooms are now temperature controlled."

"Like there's time for that. The girls are driving me nuts, asking if they can go swimming. Ally and Addy are fighting over barbies. Have you seen Crew? He's the only one I can't seem to keep track of." She shuts the door, turning to me as she rights her shirt.

Sofia points behind us. I turn, and there's Crew, sitting on the floor in the dining room, surrounded by the kitchen chairs. His knees are up, and his phone is in his face. He's got a goofy smile.

"I had asked him to put the cushions on the chairs. Apparently, he did and is now on a break." I shake my head. "Hey, Kid? Tell the girlfriend you love her, and let's go. You need to help Sofie with dinner."

"Me?" Sofia says. "Why?"

"Because cooking is one thing that will keep you both out of trouble."

"I don't cook. That's a girl job." He scoffs. "I've got to go. Love you."

"I take offense to that," Winnie complains. "What if I said us girls were done working, and you boys would be doing all the work?" Winnie snaps, stomping from the room. Sofia and Crew both watch her and then look at me.

"Men-on-pause," I say slowly. "Boy, you looking to die. If so, keep with that mouth. No misogyny in a house full of women, it will get you eaten raw." I look at my daughter. "Dinner, please?"

"Okay, daddy."

I walk away, and on my way upstairs, I find Clara, Brenton's daughter, is in the living room with six little girls. Christ, I swear to God there is something in the water in this town. The girl twin ratio is all fucked up. Though I have to say, I am guilty. Guilty of enjoying this houseful. I had wanted more kids, but Gabby refused, and I just gave up on finding someone. Then this. This beautiful, intelligent, insane woman walked into my life. Now I'm surrounded by children, and my heart is full of love, even if it's under extreme circumstances.

I've become Uncle Jarrett. I sorta like it. Coming up the stairs, I can hear Winnie. She's swearing and stomping around. I go to our room, and I see her rifling through her drawers, completely topless. I lean into the doorway with an easy smile.

"Winnie?" I say, and she stops moving but doesn't say anything. I go over to her, and as I try to hug her, she shrugs me off.

"Would you not touch me at this moment." She snaps again, pulling out a padded bra. She looks at me. "I'm pregnant."

I blink slowly as my mouth goes wet and dry simultaneously. "How? I mean, I know *how*, but did you take a test?"

She grabs her tits, and I see this little bit of cloudy liquid, which she proceeds to wipe on my face. "This is not normal. No, only I've ever done this in our little group every single time I've been pregnant. For crying out loud. This is the last thing I needed."

RESOLUTION

I wipe my face with one hand and pull her to me with the other. She fights me, pushing me back.

"Get the fuck off me! You- you did this." She's losing her shit completely.

"Winnie, my girl. You said it yourself, between menopause and your birth control, if you wound up pregnant, then the baby really wanted to be in this world. So, I guess we're about to be a baker's dozen."

"Do you understand this could be multiple? The high chances of it being so? You have a girl, and I have two girls. We're fucked."

"Maybe it'll be trip boys." I sicker, and she throws a pillow. I duck just as the door creaks open.

"Mommy, Jarrett?" Ivy's voice comes through the door. My head swivels as Winnie shoves herself into the nearest shirt.

"Hey?" I say, confused as every kid appears to be standing in our doorway, including Sofia. "What's going on?"

Ivy is holding her brother and sister's hands. "First, we want to thank you for taking care of us even when we're not the nicest of people."

"Second, we love how you love our Mommy." Comes from Iris.

Guess it's Crew's turn to speak. "Third, we love how you love us. You care more about us than our own father does. That alone means more than anything to us."

"Yeah, you even put up with us," Dante smirks. "That's a lot of crazy."

"Guys, what is going on?" I ask, a hitch in my throat. These kids are really trying to rip out my heart.

Ivy clears her little throat. "Finally, we have a serious question to ask you. Will you marry our Mommy and become our Daddy?" She lets go of her brother, and my daughter steps forward.

I watch as she slips my mother's ring from her finger. "I think this will do." She puts it in my hand. "You did good, daddy."

I choke on a tear as I look at Winnie, ring in hand.

She's got tears falling down her face as she watches our kids and me. "Are you all sure about this? *Ivy?*"

"Absolutely, I'm sorry for being such a brat before."

Winnie looks at me, and I nod. "I'd say it's too soon, but by the time we get out of this, it could be six months. Fuck it, they want me, I want you. The question is, do you want me?" I walk to her. "Winnie with God and all these kids as witness, I promise you I will be here, I will be present in this relationship, with these kids and whatever may come. You call, and I'll be there, for so long as you want me and longer still. Will you be my wife and complete my life?"

Winnie nods, "Yes." She wraps her arms over my shoulders, and we're hugged from every angle. "I love you, Jarrett Brooks."

I kiss her. I can't hold it back any longer. We may be stuck in this house for God knows how long, and it's going to be a challenge around every

RESOLUTION

corner, but this is my life. I never imagined that a New Year's resolution would change it forever...

~To New Beginnings~

About the Authors

J. Haney was born and raised in Kentucky, currently residing in Greenup County, Kentucky, with her family. She is the proud momma to Jessalyn Kristine. J. Haney's work tends to lean toward real life, drawing her readers into a world they can get lost inside.

S.I. Hayes was born and bred in New England and is currently living in Ohio. Running around Connecticut, she used all of her family and friends as inspiration for her many novels. When not writing, she can be found drawing one of many fabulous book covers or teasers.

Since meeting in 2016, the pair have embarked on the journey of a thousand tales. Keep your eyes open and a fresh pair of panties close by. You know, just in case.

Find more from J. Haney & S.I. Hayes join the mailing list-
https://landing.mailerlite.com/webforms/landing/i3s2p6

Want a chance to read it b4 it publishes? Come join our Readers Group!
https://forms.gle/RQGZck6fbXUHhdaH8

Also, by J. Haney & S.I. Hayes

(A County Fair Romance)
Wild Ride
Stolen Moments
Winter Kisses
Spring Fling
Freedom Rings
Hard Harvest
(A Sex, Drugs, and Rock Romance)
Vegas Lights
Hell in Heels
Tatted Up & Tied Down
(Working Class Beauties)
Avery
Mady
(Temptations and Troubles in Downers Grove)
The Newbie
(Navy SEAL Liaisons)
Call Sign: Baby Daddy
(The Averdeen Duet)
Tell Me Tru
(A Blue Moon Riders Tale)
Alpha Encounters: Nomity
(What If...)
Stupid Cupid
(Royals of Aeterna)
Ascension
(Welcome To...)
Hollyhock: Yuletide
(Cherry Tree Heights)
Resolution
(Stand Alone Novels)
Under His Skin
Love at Rincon Point
MisGiving Hearts

Catching Creole
Rising Star
Irish Eyes And Mafia Lies
Sweet Intentions
Island Heir
Un-Leashed
Faking It
**In Association with
(Cocky Hero Club)**
Shameless Bastard

Also, by J Haney

(Hudson Bros. PI)
An Unexpected Love

(A Heart Strings Love Affair)
Kentucky Blues
Playing House
High Convictions

(A Twist of Fate)
My Hell

Also, by S.I. Hayes

(The Roads Trilogy)
In Dreams… The Solitary Road
In Dreams… The Unavoidable Road
In Dreams… The Savage Road
(Centuries of Blood)
Becoming
(The Natural Alpha)
California Moon
(Guardians of Grigori)
Fated Binds
Midnight Run
Branded Wings
Faery Road
(Manhattanites)
Xander & Asher
(A PARKS Sector Selection)
Chasing Shadows
(Young Hearts Duet)
Penned State
(Stand Alone Novels)
Heart of Stone
Battleborn
Sweet Girls
Administrative Duties

Made in United States
Orlando, FL
29 April 2024